NIGHT OF THE LIVING DUMMY

Look for other **Goosebumps** books
by R.L. Stine:

Goosebumps®

NIGHT OF THE LIVING DUMMY

R.L. STINE

SCHOLASTIC INC.
New York Toronto London Auckland Sydney
Mexico City New Delhi Hong Kong Buenos Aires

The *Goosebumps* book series created by Parachute Press, Inc.

ISBN 0-439-56840-4

12 11 10 9 8 7 6 5 4   4 5 6 7 8/0

Printed in the U.S.A.   40

First Scholastic printing, May 1993

NIGHT OF THE LIVING DUMMY

1

"Mmmmm! Mmmm! Mmmmm!"

Kris Powell struggled to get her twin sister's attention.

Lindy Powell glanced up from the book she was reading to see what the problem was. Instead of her sister's pretty face, Lindy saw a round, pink bubble nearly the size of Kris's head.

"Nice one," Lindy said without much enthusiasm. With a sudden move, she poked the bubble and popped it.

"Hey!" Kris cried as the pink bubble gum exploded onto her cheeks and chin.

Lindy laughed. "Gotcha."

Kris angrily grabbed Lindy's paperback and slammed it shut. "Whoops — lost your place!" she exclaimed. She knew her sister hated to lose her place in a book.

Lindy grabbed the book back with a scowl. Kris struggled to pull the pink gum off her face.

"That was the biggest bubble I ever blew," she

said angrily. The gum wasn't coming off her chin.

"I've blown much bigger than that," Lindy said with a superior sneer.

"I don't *believe* you two," their mother muttered, making her way into their bedroom and dropping a neatly folded pile of laundry at the foot of Kris's bed. "You even compete over bubble gum?"

"We're not competing," Lindy muttered. She tossed back her blonde ponytail and returned her eyes to her book.

Both girls had straight blonde hair. But Lindy kept hers long, usually tying it behind her head or on one side in a ponytail. And Kris had hers cut very short.

It was a way for people to tell the twins apart, for they were nearly identical in every other way. Both had broad foreheads and round, blue eyes. Both had dimples in their cheeks when they smiled. Both blushed easily, large pink circles forming on their pale cheeks.

Both thought their noses were a little too wide. Both wished they were a little taller. Lindy's best friend, Alice, was nearly three inches taller, even though she hadn't turned twelve yet.

"Did I get it all off?" Kris asked, rubbing her chin, which was red and sticky.

"Not all," Lindy told her, glancing up. "There's some in your hair."

"Oh, great," Kris muttered. She grabbed at her

hair, but couldn't find any bubble gum.

"Gotcha again," Lindy said, laughing. "You're too easy!"

Kris uttered an angry growl. "Why are you always so mean to me?"

"Me? Mean?" Lindy looked up in wide-eyed innocence. "I'm an angel. Ask anyone."

Exasperated, Kris turned back to her mother, who was stuffing socks into a dresser drawer. "Mom, when am I going to get my own room?"

"On the Twelfth of Never," Mrs. Powell replied, grinning.

Kris groaned. "That's what you always say."

Her mother shrugged. "You know we don't have a spare inch, Kris." She turned to the bedroom window. Bright sunlight streamed through the filmy curtains. "It's a beautiful day. What are you two doing inside?"

"Mom, we're not little girls," Lindy said, rolling her eyes. "We're twelve. We're too old to go out and play."

"Did I get it all?" Kris asked, still scraping pink patches of bubble gum off her chin.

"Leave it. It improves your complexion," Lindy told her.

"I wish you girls would be nicer to each other," Mrs. Powell said with a sigh.

They suddenly heard shrill barking coming from downstairs. "What's Barky excited about now?" Mrs. Powell fretted. The little black terrier was always barking about something. "Why not take Barky for a walk?"

"Don't feel like it," Lindy muttered, nose in her book.

"What about those beautiful new bikes you got for your birthdays?" Mrs. Powell said, hands on hips. "Those bikes you just couldn't live without. You know, the ones that have been sitting in the garage since you got them."

"Okay, okay. You don't have to be sarcastic, Mom," Lindy said, closing her book. She stood up, stretched, and tossed the book onto her bed.

"You want to?" Kris asked Lindy.

"Want to what?"

"Go for a bike ride. We could ride to the play-ground, see if anyone's hanging out at school."

"You just want to see if Robby is there," Lindy said, making a face.

"So?" Kris said, blushing.

"Go on. Get some fresh air," Mrs. Powell urged. "I'll see you later. I'm off to the supermarket."

Kris peered into the dresser mirror. She had gotten most of the gum off. She brushed her short hair back with both hands. "Come on. Let's go out," she said. "Last one out is a rotten egg." She darted to the doorway, beating her sister by half a step.

As they burst out the back door, with Barky yipping shrilly behind them, the afternoon sun was high in a cloudless sky. The air was still and dry. It felt more like summer than spring.

Both girls were wearing shorts and sleeveless T-shirts. Lindy bent to pull open the garage door, then stopped. The house next door caught her eye.

"Look — they've got the walls up," she told Kris, pointing across their back yard.

"That new house is going up so quickly. It's amazing," Kris said following her sister's gaze.

The builders had knocked down the old house during the winter. The new concrete foundation had been put down in March. Lindy and Kris had walked around on it when no workers were there, trying to figure out where the different rooms would go.

And now the walls had been built. The construction suddenly looked like a real house, rising up in the midst of tall stacks of lumber, a big mound of red-brown dirt, a pile of concrete blocks, and an assortment of power saws, tools, and machinery.

"No one's working today," Lindy said.

They took a few steps toward the new house. "Who do you think will move in?" Kris wondered. "Maybe some great-looking guy our age. Maybe great-looking twin guys!"

"Yuck!" Lindy made a disgusted face. "Twin guys? How drippy can you get! I can't believe you and I are in the same family."

Kris was used to Lindy's sarcasm. Both girls liked being twins and hated being twins at the same time. Because they shared nearly everything — their looks, their clothing, their room — they were closer than most sisters ever get.

But because they were so much alike, they also managed to drive each other crazy a lot of the time.

"No one's around. Let's check out the new house," Lindy said.

Kris followed her across the yard. A squirrel, halfway up the wide trunk of a maple tree, watched them warily.

They made their way through an opening in the low shrubs that divided the two yards. Then, walking past the stacks of lumber and the tall mound of dirt, they climbed the concrete stoop.

A sheet of heavy plastic had been nailed over the opening where the front door would go. Kris pulled one end of the plastic up, and they slipped into the house.

It was dark and cool inside and had a fresh wood smell. The plaster walls were up but hadn't been painted.

"Careful," Lindy warned. "Nails." She pointed to the large nails scattered over the floor. "If you step on one, you'll get lockjaw and die."

"You wish," Kris said.

"I don't want you to die," Lindy replied. "Just get lockjaw." She snickered.

"Ha-ha," Kris said sarcastically. "This must be the living room," she said, making her way carefully across the front room to the fireplace against the back wall.

"A cathedral ceiling," Lindy said, staring up at the dark, exposed wooden beams above their heads. "Neat."

"This is bigger than our living room," Kris remarked, peering out the large picture window to the street.

"It smells great," Lindy said, taking a deep breath. "All the sawdust. It smells so piney."

They made their way through the hall and explored the kitchen. "Are those wires on?" Kris asked, pointing to a cluster of black electrical wires suspended from the ceiling beams.

"Why don't you touch one and find out?" Lindy suggested.

"You first," Kris shot back.

"The kitchen isn't very big," Lindy said, bending down to stare into the holes where the kitchen cabinets would go.

She stood up and was about to suggest they check out the upstairs when she heard a sound. "Huh?" Her eyes widened in surprise. "Is someone in here?"

Kris froze in the middle of the kitchen.

They both listened.

Silence.

Then they heard soft, rapid footsteps. Close by. Inside the house.

"Let's go!" Lindy whispered.

7

Kris was already ducking under the plastic, heading out the doorway opening. She leapt off the back stoop and started running toward their back yard.

Lindy stopped at the bottom of the stoop and turned back to the new house. "Hey — look!" she called.

A squirrel came flying out a side window. It landed on the dirt with all four feet moving and scrambled toward the maple tree in the Powells' yard.

Lindy laughed. "Just a dumb squirrel."

Kris stopped near the low shrubs. "You sure?" She hesitated, watching the windows of the new house. "That was a pretty loud squirrel."

When she turned back from the house, she was surprised to find that Lindy had disappeared.

"Hey — where'd you go?"

"Over here," Lindy called. "I see something!"

It took Kris a while to locate her sister. Lindy was half-hidden behind a large black trash Dumpster at the far end of the yard.

Kris shielded her eyes with one hand to see better. Lindy was bent over the side of the Dumpster. She appeared to be rummaging through some trash.

"What's in there?" Kris called.

Lindy was tossing things around and didn't seem to hear her.

8

"What *is* it?" Kris called, taking a few reluctant steps toward the Dumpster.

Lindy didn't reply.

Then, slowly, she pulled something out. She started to hold it up. Its arms and legs dangled down limply. Kris could see a head with brown hair.

A head? Arms and legs?

"Oh, no!" Kris cried aloud, raising her hands to her face in horror.

2

A child?

Kris uttered a silent gasp, staring in horror as Lindy lifted him out of the trash Dumpster.

She could see his face, frozen in a wide-eyed stare. His brown hair stood stiffly on top of his head. He seemed to be wearing some sort of gray suit.

His arms and legs dangled lifelessly.

"Lindy!" Kris called, her throat tight with fear. "Is it — is he . . . *alive*?"

Her heart pounding, Kris started to run to her sister. Lindy was cradling the poor thing in her arms.

"Is he alive?" Kris repeated breathlessly.

She stopped short when her sister started to laugh.

"No. Not alive!" Lindy called gleefully.

And then Kris realized that it wasn't a child after all. "A dummy!" she shrieked.

Lindy held it up. "A ventriloquist's dummy,"

she said. "Someone threw him out. Do you believe it? He's in perfect shape."

It took Lindy a while to notice that Kris was breathing hard, her face bright red. "Kris, what's your problem? Oh, wow. Did you think he was a real kid?" Lindy laughed scornfully.

"No. Of course not," Kris insisted.

Lindy held the dummy up and examined his back, looking for the string to pull to make his mouth move. "I *am* a real kid!" Lindy made him say. She was speaking in a high-pitched voice through gritted teeth, trying not to move her lips.

"Dumb," Kris said, rolling her eyes.

"I am *not* dumb. You're dumb!" Lindy made the dummy say in a high, squeaky voice. When she pulled the string in his back, the wooden lips moved up and down, clicking as they moved. She moved her hand up his back and found the control to make his painted eyes shift from side to side.

"He's probably filled with bugs," Kris said, making a disgusted face. "Throw him back, Lindy."

"No way," Lindy insisted, rubbing her hand tenderly over the dummy's wooden hair. "I'm keeping him."

"She's keeping me," she made the dummy say.

Kris stared suspiciously at the dummy. His brown hair was painted on his head. His blue eyes moved only from side to side and couldn't blink. He had bright red painted lips, curved up into an eerie smile. The lower lip had a chip on one side so that it didn't quite match the upper lip.

The dummy wore a gray, double-breasted suit over a white shirt collar. The collar wasn't attached to a shirt. Instead, the dummy's wooden chest was painted white. Big brown leather shoes were attached to the ends of his thin, dangling legs.

"My name is Slappy," Lindy made the dummy say, moving his grinning mouth up and down.

"Dumb," Kris repeated, shaking her head. "Why Slappy?"

"Come over here and I'll slap you!" Lindy made him say, trying not to move her lips.

Kris groaned. "Are we going to ride our bikes to the playground or not, Lindy?"

"Afraid poor Robby misses you?" Lindy made Slappy ask.

"Put that ugly thing down," Kris replied impatiently.

"I'm not ugly," Slappy said in Lindy's squeaky voice, sliding his eyes from side to side. "You're ugly!"

"Your lips are moving," Kris told Lindy. "You're a lousy ventriloquist."

"I'll get better," Lindy insisted.

"You mean you're really keeping it?" Kris cried.

"I like Slappy. He's cute," Lindy said, cuddling the dummy against the front of her T-shirt.

"I'm cute," she made him say. "And you're ugly."

"Shut up," Kris snapped to the dummy.

"You shut up!" Slappy replied in Lindy's tight, high-pitched voice.

"What do you want to keep him for?" Kris asked, following her sister toward the street.

"I always liked puppets," Lindy recalled. "Remember those marionettes I used to have? I played with them for hours at a time. I made up long plays with them."

"I always played with the marionettes, too," Kris remembered.

"You got the strings all tangled up," Lindy said, frowning. "You weren't any good at it."

"But what are you going to *do* with this dummy?" Kris demanded.

"I don't know. Maybe I'll work up an act," Lindy said thoughtfully, shifting Slappy to her other arm. "I'll bet I could earn some money with him. You know. Appear at kids' birthday parties. Put on shows."

"Happy birthday!" she made Slappy declare. "Hand over some money!"

Kris didn't laugh.

The two girls walked along the street in front of their house. Lindy cradled Slappy in her arms, one hand up his back.

"I think he's creepy," Kris said, kicking a large

pebble across the street. "You should put him back in the Dumpster."

"No way," Lindy insisted.

"No way," she made Slappy say, shaking his head, his glassy blue eyes moving from side to side. "I'll put *you* in the Dumpster!"

"Slappy sure is mean," Kris remarked, frowning at Lindy.

Lindy laughed. "Don't look at me," she teased. "Complain to Slappy."

Kris scowled.

"You're jealous," Lindy said. "Because I found him and you didn't."

Kris started to protest, but they both heard voices. Kris looked up to see the two Marshall kids from down the block running toward them. They were cute, red-headed kids that Lindy and Kris sometimes baby-sat for.

"What's that?" Amy Marshall asked, pointing at Slappy.

"Does he talk?" her younger brother, Ben, asked, staying several feet away, an uncertain expression on his freckled face.

"Hi, I'm Slappy!" Lindy made the dummy call out. She cradled Slappy in one arm, making him sit up straight, his arms dangling at his sides.

"Where'd you get him?" Amy asked.

"Do his eyes move?" Ben asked, still hanging back.

"Do *your* eyes move?" Slappy asked Ben.

14

Both Marshall kids laughed. Ben forgot his reluctance. He stepped up and grabbed Slappy's hand.

"Ouch! Not so hard!" Slappy cried.

Ben dropped the hand with a gasp. Then he and Amy collapsed in gleeful laughter.

"Ha-ha-ha-ha!" Lindy made Slappy laugh, tilting his head back and opening his mouth wide.

The two kids thought that was a riot. They laughed even harder.

Pleased by the response she was getting, Lindy glanced at her sister. Kris was sitting on the curb, cradling her head in her hands, a dejected look on her face.

She's jealous, Lindy realized. Kris sees that the kids really like Slappy and that I'm getting all the attention. And she's totally jealous.

I'm *definitely* keeping Slappy! Lindy told herself, secretly pleased at her little triumph.

She stared into the dummy's bright blue painted eyes. To her surprise, the dummy seemed to be staring back at her, a twinkle of sunlight in his eyes, his grin wide and knowing.

3

"Who was that on the phone?" Mr. Powell asked, shoveling another forkful of spaghetti into his mouth.

Lindy slipped back into her place at the table. "It was Mrs. Marshall. Down the block."

"Does she want you to baby-sit?" Mrs. Powell asked, reaching for the salad bowl. She turned to Kris. "Don't you want any salad?"

Kris wiped spaghetti sauce off her chin with her napkin. "Maybe later."

"No," Lindy answered. "She wants me to perform. At Amy's birthday party. With Slappy."

"Your first job," Mr. Powell said, a smile crossing his slender face.

"Amy and Ben liked Slappy so much, they insisted on him," Lindy said. "Mrs. Marshall is going to pay me twenty dollars."

"That's great!" their mother exclaimed. She passed the salad bowl across the table to her husband.

It had been a week since Lindy rescued Slappy from the trash Dumpster. Every day after school, she had spent hours up in her room rehearsing with him, working on his voice, practicing not moving her lips, thinking up jokes to perform with him.

Kris kept insisting the whole thing was dumb. "I can't believe you're being such a nerd," she told her sister. She refused to be an audience for Lindy's routines.

But when Lindy brought Slappy into school on Friday, Kris's attitude began to change. A group of kids had gathered around Lindy outside her locker.

As Lindy made Slappy talk for them, Kris watched from down the hall. She's going to make a total fool of herself, Kris thought.

But to her surprise, the kids hooted and howled. They thought Slappy was a riot. Even Robby Martin, the guy Kris had had a crush on for two years, thought Lindy was terrific.

Watching Robby laugh along with the other kids made Kris think hard. Becoming a ventriloquist might be fun.

And profitable. Lindy was going to earn twenty dollars at the Marshalls' birthday party. And when word got around, she'd probably perform at a lot of parties and earn even more money.

After dinner that evening, Lindy and Kris washed and dried the dishes. Then Lindy asked her parents if she could practice her new comedy routine on them. She hurried up to her room to get Slappy.

Mr. and Mrs. Powell took a seat on the living room couch. "Maybe Lindy will be a TV star," Mrs. Powell said.

"Maybe," Mr. Powell agreed, settling back on the couch, a pleased smile on his face. Barky yapped and climbed between Mr. and Mrs. Powell, his tiny stub of a tail wagging furiously.

"You know you're not allowed on the couch," Mrs. Powell said, sighing. But she made no move to push Barky off.

Kris sat down away from the others, on the floor by the steps, cradling her chin in her hands.

"You're looking glum this evening," her father remarked.

"Can I get a dummy, too?" Kris asked. She hadn't really planned to say it. The question just popped out of her mouth.

Lindy came back into the room, carrying Slappy around the waist. "Ready?" she asked. She pulled a dining room chair into the center of the living room and sat down on it.

"Well, can I?" Kris repeated.

"You really want one, too?" Mrs. Powell asked, surprised.

"Want *what*?" Lindy asked, confused.

"Kris says she wants a dummy, too," Mrs. Powell reported.

"No way," Lindy said heatedly. "Why do you want to be such a copycat?"

"It looks like fun," Kris replied, her cheeks turning bright pink. "If you can do it, I can do it, too," she added shrilly.

"You always copy everything I do," Lindy protested angrily. "Why don't you find something of your own for once? Go upstairs and work on your junk jewelry collection. That's *your* hobby. Let *me* be the ventriloquist."

"Girls" — Mr. Powell started, raising a hand for quiet — "please, don't fight over a dummy."

"I really think I'd be better at it," Kris said. "I mean, Lindy isn't very funny."

"Everyone thinks I'm funny," Lindy insisted.

"That's not very nice, Kris," Mrs. Powell scolded.

"Well, I just think if Lindy has one, I should be able to have one, too," Kris said to her parents.

"Copycat," Lindy repeated, shaking her head. "You've been putting me down all week. You said it was nerdy. But I know why you changed your mind. You're upset because I'm going to earn some money and you're not."

"I really wish you two wouldn't argue about *everything*," Mr. Powell said disgustedly.

19

"Well, can I have a dummy?" Kris asked him.

"They're expensive," Mr. Powell replied, glancing at his wife. "A good one will cost more than a hundred dollars. I really don't think we can afford to buy one now."

"Why don't you both share Slappy?" Mrs. Powell suggested.

"Huh?" Lindy's mouth dropped open in protest.

"You two always share everything," Mrs. Powell continued. "So why don't you share Slappy?"

"But, Mom — " Lindy whined unhappily.

"Excellent idea," Mr. Powell interrupted. He motioned to Kris. "Try it out. After you share him for a while, I'm sure one of you will lose interest in him. Maybe even both of you."

Kris climbed to her feet and walked over to Lindy. She reached out for the dummy. "I don't mind sharing," she said quietly, searching her sister's eyes for approval of the idea. "Can I hold him for just a second?"

Lindy held onto Slappy tightly.

Suddenly the dummy's head tilted back and his mouth opened wide. *"Beat it, Kris!"* he snarled in a harsh raspy voice. *"Get lost, you stupid moron!"*

Before Kris could back away, Slappy's wooden hand shot up, and he slapped her hard across the face.

4

"Ow!"

Kris screamed and raised her hand to her cheek, which was bright pink. She stepped back. "Stop it, Lindy! That *hurt*!"

"Me?" Lindy cried. "I didn't do it! Slappy did!"

"Don't be dumb," Kris protested, rubbing her cheek. "You really hurt me."

"But I didn't do it!" Lindy cried. She turned Slappy's face toward her. "Why were you so rude to Kris?"

Mr. Powell jumped up from the couch. "Stop acting dumb and apologize to your sister," he ordered.

Lindy bowed Slappy's head. "I'm sorry," she made the dummy say.

"No. In your own voice," Mr. Powell insisted, crossing his arms in front of his chest. "Slappy didn't hurt Kris. You did."

21

"Okay, okay," Lindy muttered, blushing. She avoided Kris's angry stare. "I'm sorry. Here." She dumped Slappy into Kris's arms.

Kris was so surprised, she nearly dropped the dummy. Slappy was heavier than she'd imagined.

"Now what am I supposed to do with him?" Kris asked Lindy.

Lindy shrugged and crossed the room to the couch, where she dropped down beside her mother.

"Why'd you make such a fuss?" Mrs. Powell whispered, leaning close to Lindy. "That was so babyish."

Lindy blushed. "Slappy is *mine*! Why can't something be mine for once?"

"Sometimes you girls are so nice to each other, and sometimes . . ." Mrs. Powell's voice trailed off.

Mr. Powell took a seat on the padded arm of the chair across the room.

"How do I make his mouth work?" Kris asked, tilting the dummy upside down to examine its back.

"There's a string in his back, inside the slit in his jacket," Lindy told her grudgingly. "You just pull it."

I don't want Kris to work Slappy, Lindy thought unhappily.

I don't want to share Slappy.

Why can't I have something that just belongs

to me? Why do I have to share everything with her?

Why does Kris always want to copy me?

She gritted her teeth and waited for her anger to fade.

Later that night, Kris sat straight up in bed. She'd had a bad dream.

I was being chased, she remembered, her heart still pounding. Chased by what? By whom?

She couldn't remember.

She glanced around the shadowy room, waiting for her heartbeat to return to normal. The room felt hot and stuffy, even though the window was open and the curtains were fluttering.

Lindy lay sound asleep on her side in the twin bed next to Kris's. She was snoring softly, her lips slightly parted, her long hair falling loose about her face.

Kris glanced at the clock-radio on the bed table between the two twin beds. It was nearly three in the morning.

Even though she was now wide awake, the nightmare wouldn't completely fade away. She still felt uncomfortable, a little frightened, as if she were still being chased by someone or something. The back of her neck felt hot and prickly.

She turned and fluffed up her pillow, propping it higher on the headboard. As she lay back on it, something caught her eye.

Someone sitting in the chair in front of the bedroom window. Someone staring at her.

After a sharp intake of breath, she realized it was Slappy.

Yellow moonlight poured over him, making his staring eyes glow. He was sitting up in the chair, tilted to the right at a slight angle, one arm resting on the slender arm of the chair.

His mouth locked in a wide, mocking grin, his eyes seemed to be staring right at Kris.

Kris stared back, studying the dummy's expression in the eerie yellow moonlight. Then, without thinking, without even realizing what she was doing, she climbed silently out of bed.

Her foot got tangled in the bedsheet and she nearly tripped. Kicking the sheet away, she made her way quickly across the room to the window.

Slappy stared up at her as her shadow fell over him. His grin seemed to grow wider as Kris leaned closer.

A gust of wind made the soft curtains flutter against her face. Kris pushed them away and peered down at the dummy's painted head.

She reached a hand out and rubbed his wooden hair, shining in the moonlight. His head felt warm, warmer than she'd imagined.

Kris quickly jerked her hand away.

What was that sound?

Had Slappy snickered? Had he laughed at her? No. Of course not.

Kris realized she was breathing hard.

Why am I so freaked out by this stupid dummy? she thought.

In the bed behind her, Lindy made a gurgling sound and rolled onto her back.

Kris stared hard into Slappy's big eyes, gleaming in the light from the window. She waited for him to blink or to roll his eyes from side to side.

She suddenly felt foolish.

He's just a stupid wooden dummy, she told herself.

She reached out and pushed him over.

The stiff body swung to the side. The hard head made a soft *clonk* as it hit the wooden arm of the chair.

Kris stared down at him, feeling strangely satisfied, as if she'd somehow taught him a lesson.

The curtains rustled against her face again. She pushed them away.

Feeling sleepy, she started back to bed.

She had only gone one step when Slappy reached up and grabbed her wrist.

5

"Oh!" As the hand tightened around her wrist, Kris cried out and spun around.

To her surprise, Lindy was crouched beside her. Lindy had a tight grip on Kris's wrist.

Kris jerked her hand from Lindy's grasp.

Moonlight through the window lit up Lindy's devilish grin. "Gotcha again!" she declared.

"You didn't scare me!" Kris insisted. But her voice came out a trembling whisper.

"You jumped a mile!" Lindy exclaimed gleefully. "You really thought the dummy grabbed you."

"Did not!" Kris replied. She hurried to her bed.

"What were you doing up, anyway?" Lindy demanded. "Were you messing with Slappy?"

"No. I . . . uh . . . had a bad dream," Kris told her. "I just went to look out the window."

Lindy snickered. "You should've seen the look on your face."

"I'm going back to sleep. Leave me alone," Kris

snapped. She pulled the covers up to her chin.

Lindy pushed the dummy back to a sitting position. Then she returned to her bed, still chuckling over the scare she'd given her sister.

Kris rearranged her pillows, then glanced across the room to the window. The dummy's face was half covered in shadow now. But the eyes glowed as if he were alive. And they stared into hers as if they were trying to tell her something.

Why does he have to grin like that? Kris asked herself, trying to rub away the prickly feeling on the back of her neck.

She pulled up the sheet, settled into the bed, and turned on her side, away from the wide, staring eyes.

But even with her back turned, she could feel them gazing at her. Even with her eyes closed and the covers pulled up to her head, she could picture the shadowy, distorted grin, the unblinking eyes. Staring at her. Staring. Staring.

She drifted into an uncomfortable sleep, drifted into another dark nightmare. Someone was chasing her. Someone very evil was chasing her.

But who?

On Monday afternoon, Lindy and Kris both stayed after school to rehearse for the spring concert. It was nearly five when they arrived home, and they were surprised to see their dad's car in the driveway.

"You're home so early!" Kris exclaimed, finding him in the kitchen helping their mother prepare dinner.

"I'm leaving tomorrow for a sales conference in Portland," Mr. Powell explained, peeling an onion over the sink with a small paring knife. "So I only worked half a day today."

"What's for dinner?" Lindy asked.

"Meat loaf," Mrs. Powell replied, "if your father ever gets the onion peeled."

"There's a trick to not crying when you peel an onion," Mr. Powell said, tears rolling down his cheeks. "Wish I knew it."

"How was chorus rehearsal?" Mrs. Powell asked, kneading a big ball of red ground beef in her hands.

"Boring," Lindy complained, opening the refrigerator and taking out a can of Coke.

"Yeah. We're doing all these Russian and Yugoslavian songs," Kris said. "They're so sad. They're all about sheep or something. We don't really know what they're about. There's no translation."

Mr. Powell rushed to the sink and began splashing cold water on his red, runny eyes. "I can't take this!" he wailed. He tossed the half-peeled onion back to his wife.

"Crybaby," she muttered, shaking her head.

Kris headed up the stairs to drop her backpack in her room. She tossed it onto the desk she shared with Lindy, then turned to go back downstairs.

But something by the window caught her eye. Spinning around, she gasped.

"Oh, no!" The startled cry escaped her lips.

Kris raised her hands to her cheeks and stared in disbelief.

Slappy was propped up in the chair in front of the window, grinning at her with his usual wide-eyed stare. And seated beside him was another dummy, also grinning at her.

And they were holding hands.

"What's going on here?" Kris cried aloud.

6

"Do you like him?"

At first, Kris thought that Slappy had asked the question.

She gaped in stunned disbelief.

"Well? What do you think of him?"

It took Kris a long moment to realize that the voice was coming from behind her. She turned to find her father standing in the doorway, still dabbing at his eyes with a wet dishtowel.

"The — the new dummy?" Kris stammered.

"He's for you," Mr. Powell said, stepping into the room, the wet towel pressed against both eyes.

"Really?" Kris hurried over to the chair and picked the new dummy up to examine him.

"There's a tiny pawnshop on the corner across from my office," Mr. Powell said, lowering the towel. "I was walking past and, believe it or not, this guy was in the window. He was cheap, too. I think the pawnbroker was glad to get rid of him."

"He's . . . cute," Kris said, searching for the right word. "He looks just like Lindy's dummy, except his hair is bright red, not brown."

"Probably made by the same company," Mr. Powell said.

"His clothes are better than Slappy's," Kris said, holding the dummy out at arm's length to get a good view. "I hate that stupid gray suit on Lindy's dummy."

The new dummy wore blue denim jeans and a red-and-green flannel shirt. And instead of the formal-looking, shiny brown shoes, he had white high-top sneakers on his feet.

"So you like him?" Mr. Powell asked, smiling.

"I *love* him!" Kris cried happily. She crossed the room and gave her dad a hug.

Then she picked up the dummy and ran out of the room, down the stairs, and into the kitchen. "Hey, everybody! Meet Mr. Wood!" she declared happily, holding the grinning dummy up in front of her.

Barky yapped excitedly, leaping up to nip at the dummy's sneakers. Kris pulled her dummy away.

"Hey!" Lindy cried in surprise. "Where'd you get that?"

"From Daddy," Kris said, her grin wider than the dummy's. "I'm going to start practicing with him after dinner, and I'm going to be a better ventriloquist than you."

"Kris!" Mrs. Powell scolded. "Everything isn't a competition, you know!"

"I already have a job with Slappy," Lindy said with a superior sneer. "And you're just getting started. You're just a beginner."

"Mr. Wood is much better-looking than Slappy," Kris said, mirroring her twin's sneer. "Mr. Wood is cool-looking. That gray suit on your dummy is the pits."

"You think that ratty old shirt is cool-looking?" Lindy scoffed, making a disgusted face. "Yuck. That old dummy probably has worms!"

"*You* have worms!" Kris exclaimed.

"Your dummy won't be funny," Lindy said nastily, "because you don't have a sense of humor."

"Oh, yeah?" Kris replied, tossing Mr. Wood over her shoulder. "I *must* have a sense of humor. I put up with *you*, don't I?"

"Copycat! Copycat!" Lindy cried angrily.

"Out of the kitchen!" Mrs. Powell ordered with an impatient shriek. "Out! Get out! You two are impossible! The dummies have better personalities than either of you!"

"Thanks, Mom," Kris said sarcastically.

"Call me for dinner," Lindy called back. "I'm going upstairs to practice my act with Slappy for the birthday party on Saturday."

It was the next afternoon, and Kris was sitting at the dressing table she shared with Lindy. Kris rummaged in the jewelry box and pulled out another string of brightly colored beads. She slipped them over her head and untangled them from the other three strands of beads she was wearing. Then she gazed at herself in the mirror, shaking her head to better see the long, dangly earrings.

I love my junk jewelry collection, she thought, digging into the depths of the wooden jewelry box to see what other treasures she could pull out.

Lindy had no interest in the stuff. But Kris could spend hours trying on the beads, fingering the dozens of little charms, running her fingers over the plastic bracelets, jangling the earrings. Her jewelry collection always cheered her up.

She shook her head again, making the long earrings jangle. A knock on the bedroom door made her spin around.

"Hey, Kris, how's it going?" Her friend Cody Matthews stepped into the room. He had straight, white-blond hair, and pale gray eyes in a slender, serious face. Cody always looked as if he were deep in thought.

"You ride your bike over?" Kris asked, removing several strands of beads at once and tossing them into the jewelry box.

"No. Walked," Cody replied. "Why'd you call? You just want to hang out?"

"No." Kris jumped to her feet. She walked over to the chair by the window and grabbed up Mr. Wood. "I want to practice my act."

Cody groaned. "I'm the guinea pig?"

"No. The audience. Come on."

She led him out to the bent old maple tree in the middle of her back yard. The afternoon sun was just beginning to lower itself in the clear, spring-blue sky.

She raised one foot against the tree trunk and propped Mr. Wood on her knee. Cody sprawled on his back in the shade. "Tell me if this is funny," she instructed.

"Okay. Shoot," Cody replied, narrowing his eyes in concentration.

Kris turned Mr. Wood to face her. "How are you today?" she asked him.

"Pretty good. Knock wood," she made the dummy say.

She waited for Cody to laugh, but he didn't. "Was that funny?" she asked.

"Kinda," he replied without enthusiasm. "Keep going."

"Okay." Kris lowered her head so that she was face-to-face with her dummy. "Mr. Wood," she said, "why were you standing in front of the mirror with your eyes closed?"

"Well," answered the dummy in a high-pitched, squeaky voice, "I wanted to see what I look like when I'm asleep!"

Kris tilted the dummy's head back and made him look as if he were laughing. "How about that joke?" she asked Cody.

34

Cody shrugged. "Better, I guess."

"Aw, you're no help!" Kris screamed angrily. She lowered her arms, and Mr. Wood crumpled onto her lap. "You're supposed to tell me if it's funny or not."

"I guess *not*," Cody said thoughtfully.

Kris groaned. "I need some good joke books," she said. "That's all. Some good joke books with some really funny jokes. Then I'd be ready to perform. Because I'm a pretty good ventriloquist, right?"

"I guess," Cody replied, pulling up a handful of grass and letting the moist, green blades sift through his fingers.

"Well, I don't move my lips very much, *do* I?" Kris demanded.

"Not too much," Cody allowed. "But you don't really throw your voice."

"No one can throw her voice," Kris told him. "It's just an illusion. You make people *think* you're throwing your voice. You don't *really* throw it."

"Oh," Cody said, pulling up another handful of grass.

Kris tried out several more jokes. "What do you think?" she asked Cody.

"I think I have to go home," Cody said. He tossed a handful of grass at her.

Kris brushed the green blades off Mr. Wood's wooden head. She rubbed her hand gently over the dummy's painted red hair. "You're hurting

35

Mr. Wood's feelings," she told Cody.

Cody climbed to his feet. "Why do you want to mess with that thing, anyway?" he asked, pushing his white-blond hair back off his forehead.

"Because it's fun," Kris replied.

"Is that the real reason?" Cody demanded.

"Well . . . I guess I want to show Lindy that I'm better at it than she is."

"You two are *weird*!" Cody declared. "See you in school." He gave her a little wave, then turned and headed for his home down the block.

Kris pulled down the blankets and climbed into bed. Pale moonlight filtered in through the bedroom window.

Yawning, she glanced at the clock-radio. Nearly ten. She could hear Lindy brushing her teeth in the bathroom across the hall.

Why does Lindy always hum when she brushes her teeth? Kris wondered. How can one twin sister do so many annoying things?

She gave Mr. Wood one last glance. He was propped in the chair in front of the window, his hands carefully placed in his lap, his white sneakers hanging over the chair edge.

He looks like a real person, Kris thought sleepily.

Tomorrow I'm going to check out some good joke books from the library at school. I can be funnier than Lindy. I *know* I can.

She settled back sleepily on her pillow. I'll be asleep as soon as we turn off the lights, she thought.

A few seconds later, Lindy entered the room, wearing her nightshirt and carrying Slappy under one arm. "You asleep?" she asked Kris.

"Almost," Kris replied, yawning loudly. "I've been studying for the math final all night. Where've you been?"

"Over at Alice's," Lindy told her, setting Slappy down in the chair beside Mr. Wood. "Some kids were over, and I practiced my act for them. They laughed so hard, I thought they'd split a gut. When Slappy and I did our rap routine, Alice spit her chocolate milk out her nose. What a riot!"

"That's nice," Kris said without enthusiasm. "Guess you and Slappy are ready for Amy's birthday party on Saturday."

"Yeah," Lindy replied. She placed Slappy's arm around Mr. Wood's shoulder. "They look so cute together," she said. Then she noticed the clothing neatly draped over the desk chair. "What's that?" she asked Kris.

Kris raised her head from the pillow to see what her sister was pointing at. "My outfit for tomorrow," she told her. "We're having a dress-up party in Miss Finch's class. It's a farewell party. For Margot. You know. The student teacher."

Lindy stared at the clothes. "Your Betsey Johnson skirt? Your silk blouse?"

"We're supposed to get really dressed up," Kris said, yawning. "Can we go to sleep now?"

"Yeah. Sure." Lindy made her way to her bed, sat down, and clicked off the bed-table lamp. "Are you getting any better with Mr. Wood?" she asked, climbing between the sheets.

Kris was stung by the question. It was such an obvious put-down. "Yeah. I'm getting really good. I did some stuff for Cody. Out in the back yard. Cody laughed so hard, he couldn't breathe. Really. He was holding his sides. He said Mr. Wood and I should be on TV."

"Really?" Lindy replied after a long moment's hesitation. "That's weird. I never thought Cody had much of a sense of humor. He's always so grim. I don't think I've ever seen him laugh."

"Well, he was laughing at Mr. Wood and me," Kris insisted, wishing she were a better liar.

"Awesome," Lindy muttered. "I can't wait to see your act."

Neither can I, Kris thought glumly.

A few seconds later, they were both asleep.

Their mother's voice, calling from downstairs, awoke them at seven the next morning. Bright, morning-orange sunlight poured in through the window. Kris could hear birds chirping happily in the old maple tree.

"Rise and shine! Rise and shine!" Every morning, Mrs. Powell shouted up the same words.

Kris rubbed the sleep from her eyes, then stretched her arms high over her head. She glanced across the room, then uttered a quiet gasp. "Hey — what's going on?" She reached across to Lindy's bed and shook Lindy by the shoulder. "What's going on?"

"Huh?" Lindy, startled, sat straight up.

"What's the joke? Where is he?" Kris demanded.

"Huh?"

Kris pointed to the chair across the room.

Sitting straight up in the chair, Slappy grinned back at them, bathed in morning sunlight.

But Mr. Wood was gone.

7

Kris blinked several times and pushed herself up in bed with both hands. Her left hand tingled. She must have been sleeping on it, she realized.

"What? What's wrong?" Lindy asked, her voice fogged with sleep.

"Where's Mr. Wood?" Kris demanded impatiently. "Where'd you put him?"

"Huh? Put him?" Lindy struggled to focus her eyes. She saw Slappy sitting stiffly on the chair across the room. By himself.

"It's not funny," Kris snapped. She climbed out of bed, pulled down the hem of her nightshirt, and made her way quickly to the chair in front of the window. "Don't you ever get tired of playing stupid jokes?"

"Jokes? Huh?" Lindy lowered her feet to the floor.

Kris bent down to search the floor under the chair. Then she moved to the foot of the bed and got down on her knees to search under both twin beds.

"Where *is* he, Lindy?" she asked angrily, on her knees at the foot of the bed. "I don't think this is funny. I really don't."

"Well, neither do I," Lindy insisted, standing up and stretching.

Kris climbed to her feet. Her eyes went wide as she spotted the missing dummy.

"Oh!"

Lindy followed her sister's startled gaze.

Mr. Wood grinned at them from the doorway. He appeared to be standing, his skinny legs bent at an awkward angle.

He was wearing Kris's dress-up clothes, the Betsey Johnson skirt and the silk blouse.

Her mouth wide open in surprise, Kris made her way quickly to the doorway. She immediately saw that the dummy wasn't really standing on his own. He had been propped up, the doorknob shoved into the opening in his back.

She grabbed the dummy by the waist and pulled him away from the door. "My blouse. It's all wrinkled," she cried, holding it so Lindy could see. She narrowed her eyes angrily at her sister. "This was so obnoxious of you, Lindy."

"Me?" Lindy shrieked. "I swear, Kris, I didn't do it. I slept like a rock last night. I didn't move. I didn't get up till you woke me. I didn't do it. Really!"

41

Kris stared hard at her sister, then lowered her eyes to the dummy.

In her blouse and skirt, Mr. Wood grinned up at her, as if enjoying her bewilderment.

"Well, Mr. Wood," Kris said aloud, "I guess you put on my clothes and walked to the door all by yourself!"

Lindy started to say something. But their mother's voice from downstairs interrupted. "Are you girls going to school today? Where *are* you? You're late!"

"Coming!" Kris called down, casting an angry glance at Lindy. She carefully set Mr. Wood down on his back on her bed and pulled her skirt and blouse off him. She looked up to see Lindy making a mad dash across the hall to be first in the bathroom.

Sighing, Kris stared down at Mr. Wood. The dummy grinned up at her, a mischievous grin.

"Well? What's going on?" she asked the dummy. "I didn't dress you up and move you. And Lindy swears *she* didn't do it."

But if we didn't do it, she thought, *who did?*

8

"Tilt his head forward," Lindy instructed. "That's it. If you bounce him up and down a little, it'll make it look like he's laughing."

Kris obediently bounced Mr. Wood on her lap, making him laugh.

"Don't move his mouth so much," Lindy told her.

"I think you're both crazy," Lindy's friend Alice said.

"So what else is new?" Cody joked.

All four of them were sitting in a small patch of shade under the bent old maple tree in the Powells' back yard. It was a hot Saturday afternoon, the sun high in a pale blue sky, streaks of yellow light filtering down through the shifting leaves above their heads.

Barky sniffed busily around the yard, his little tail wagging nonstop.

Kris sat on a folding chair, which leaned back

43

against the gnarled tree trunk. She had Mr. Wood on her lap.

Lindy and Alice stood at the edge of the shade, their hands crossed over their chests, watching Kris's performance with frowns of concentration on their faces.

Alice was a tall, skinny girl, with straight black hair down to her shoulders, a snub nose, and a pretty, heart-shaped mouth. She was wearing white shorts and a bright blue midriff top.

Cody was sprawled on his back in the grass, his hands behind his head, a long blade of grass between his teeth.

Kris was trying to show off her ventriloquist skills. But Lindy kept interrupting with "helpful" suggestions. When she wasn't making suggestions, Lindy was nervously glancing at her watch. She didn't want to be late for her job at Amy's birthday party at two o'clock.

"I think you're way weird," Alice told Lindy.

"Hey, no way," Lindy replied. "Slappy is a lot of fun. And I'm going to make a lot of money with him. And maybe I'll be a comedy star or something when I'm older." She glanced at her watch again.

"Well, everyone at school thinks that both of you are weird," Alice said, swatting a fly off her bare arm.

"Who cares?" Lindy replied sharply. "They're all weird, too."

"And so are you," Kris made Mr. Wood say.

"I could see your lips move," Lindy told Kris.

Kris rolled her eyes. "Give me a break. You've been giving me a hard time all morning."

"Just trying to help," Lindy said. "You don't have to be so defensive, do you?"

Kris uttered an angry growl.

"Was that your stomach?" she made Mr. Wood say.

Cody laughed.

"At least *one* person thinks you're funny," Lindy said dryly. "But if you want to do parties, you really should get some better jokes."

Kris let the dummy slump to her lap. "I can't find any good joke books," she said dejectedly. "Where do you find your jokes?"

A superior sneer formed on Lindy's face. She tossed her long hair behind her shoulder. "I make up my own jokes," she replied snootily.

"You *are* a joke!" Cody said.

"Ha-ha. Remind me to laugh later," Lindy said sarcastically.

"I can't believe you don't have *your* dummy out here," Alice told Lindy. "I mean, don't you want to rehearse for the party?"

"No need," Lindy replied. "I've got my act down. I don't want to over-rehearse."

Kris groaned loudly.

"Some of the other parents are staying at the birthday party to watch Slappy and me," Lindy continued, ignoring Kris's sarcasm. "If the kids

45

like me, their parents might hire me for *their* parties."

"Maybe you and Kris should do an act together," Alice suggested. "That could be really awesome."

"Yeah. What an act! Then there'd be *four* dummies!" Cody joked.

Alice was the only one to laugh.

Lindy made a face at Cody. "That might actually be fun," she said thoughtfully. And then she added, "When Kris is ready."

Kris drew in her breath and prepared to make an angry reply.

But before she could say anything, Lindy grabbed Mr. Wood from her hands. "Let me give you a few pointers," Lindy said, putting one foot on Kris's folding chair and arranging Mr. Wood on her lap. "You have to hold him up straighter, like this."

"Hey — give him back," Kris demanded, reaching for her dummy.

As she reached up, Mr. Wood suddenly lowered his head until he was staring down at her. *"You're a jerk!"* he rasped in Kris's face, speaking in a low, throaty growl.

"Huh?" Kris pulled back in surprise.

"You're a stupid jerk!" Mr. Wood repeated nastily in the same harsh growl.

"Lindy — stop it!" Kris cried.

Cody and Alice both stared in openmouthed surprise.

"*Stupid moron! Get lost! Get lost, stupid jerk!*" the dummy rasped in Kris's face.

"Whoa!" Cody exclaimed.

"Make him stop!" Kris screamed at her sister.

"I can't!" Lindy cried in a trembling voice. Her face became pale, her eyes wide with fear. "I can't make him stop, Kris! He — he's speaking for himself!"

9

The dummy glared at Kris, its grin ugly and evil.

"I — I can't make him stop. I'm not doing it," Lindy cried. Tugging with all her might, she pulled Mr. Wood out of Kris's face.

Cody and Alice flashed each other bewildered glances.

Frightened, Kris raised herself from the folding chair and backed up against the tree trunk. "He — he's talking on his own?" She stared hard at the grinning dummy.

"I — I think so. I'm . . . all mixed up!" Lindy declared, her cheeks bright pink.

Barky yipped and jumped on Lindy's legs, trying to get her attention. But she kept her gaze on Kris's frightened face.

"This is a joke — right?" Cody asked hopefully.

"What's going on?" Alice demanded, her arms crossed in front of her chest.

Ignoring them, Lindy handed Mr. Wood back

to Kris. "Here. Take him. He's yours. Maybe *you* can control him."

"But, Lindy — " Kris started to protest.

Lindy glared at her watch. "Oh, no! The party! I'm late!" Shaking her head, she took off toward the house. "Later!" she called without looking back.

"But Lindy — " Kris called.

The kitchen door slammed behind Lindy.

Holding Mr. Wood by the shoulders, Kris lowered her eyes to his face. He grinned up at her, a devilish grin, his eyes staring intently into hers.

Kris swung easily, leaning back and raising her feet into the air. The chains squeaked with every swing. The old back yard swingset, half covered with rust, hadn't been used much in recent years.

The early evening sun was lowering itself behind the house. The aroma of a roasting chicken floated out from the kitchen window. Kris could hear her mother busy in the kitchen preparing dinner.

Barky yapped beneath her. Kris dropped her feet to the ground and stopped the swing to avoid kicking him. "Dumb dog. Don't you know you could get hurt?"

She looked up to see Lindy come running up the driveway, holding Slappy under her arm. From the smile on Lindy's face, Kris knew at once that the birthday party had been a triumph. But she had to ask anyway. "How'd it go?"

"It was awesome!" Lindy exclaimed. "Slappy and I were *great*!"

Kris pulled herself off the swing and forced a smile to her face. "That's nice," she offered.

"The kids thought we were a riot!" Lindy continued. She pulled Slappy up. "Didn't they, Slappy?"

"They liked me. Hated you!" Slappy declared in Lindy's high-pitched voice.

Kris forced a laugh. "I'm glad it went okay," she said, trying hard to be a good sport.

"I did a sing-along with Slappy, and it went over really well. Then Slappy and I did our rap routine. What a hit!" Lindy gushed.

She's spreading it on a little thick, Kris thought bitterly. Kris couldn't help feeling jealous.

"The kids all lined up to talk to Slappy," Lindy continued. "Didn't they, Slappy?"

"Everyone loved me," she made the dummy say. "Where's my share of the loot?"

"So you got paid twenty dollars?" Kris asked, kicking at a clump of weeds.

"Twenty-five," Lindy replied. "Amy's mom said I was so good, she'd pay me extra. Oh. And guess what else? You know Mrs. Evans? The woman who always wears the leopardskin pants? You know — Anna's mom? She asked me to do Anna's party next Sunday. She's going to pay me *thirty* dollars! I'm going to be rich!"

"Wow. Thirty dollars," Kris muttered, shaking her head.

"I get twenty. You get ten," Lindy made Slappy say.

"I have to go tell Mom the good news!" Lindy said. "What have you been doing all afternoon?"

"Well, after you left, I was pretty upset," Kris replied, following Lindy to the house. "You know. About Mr. Wood. I — I put him upstairs. Alice and Cody went home. Then Mom and I went to the mall."

His tail wagging furiously, Barky ran right over their feet, nearly tripping both of them. "Barky, look out!" Lindy yelled.

"Oh. I nearly forgot," Kris said, stopping on the back stoop. "Something good happened."

Lindy stopped, too. "Something good?"

"Yeah. I ran into Mrs. Berman at the mall." Mrs. Berman was their music teacher and organizer of the spring concert.

"Thrills," Lindy replied sarcastically.

"And Mrs. Berman asked if Mr. Wood and I wanted to be master of ceremonies for the spring concert." Kris smiled at her sister.

Lindy swallowed hard. "She asked *you* to host the concert?"

"Yeah. I get to perform with Mr. Wood in front

51

of everyone!" Kris gushed happily. She saw a flash of jealousy on Lindy's face, which made her even happier.

Lindy pulled open the screen door. "Well, good luck," she said dryly. "With that weird dummy of yours, you'll *need* it."

Dinner was spent talking about Lindy's performance at Amy Marshall's birthday party. Lindy and Mrs. Powell chatted excitedly. Kris ate in silence.

"At first I thought the whole thing was strange, I have to admit," Mrs. Powell said, scooping ice cream into bowls for dessert. "I just couldn't believe you'd be interested in ventriloquism, Lindy. But I guess you have a flair for it. I guess you have some talent."

Lindy beamed. Mrs. Powell normally wasn't big on compliments.

"I found a book in the school library about ventriloquism," Lindy said. "It had some pretty good tips in it. It even had a comedy routine to perform." She glanced at Kris. "But I like making up my own jokes better."

"You should watch your sister's act," Mrs. Powell told Kris, handing her a bowl of ice cream. "I mean, you could probably pick up some pointers for the concert at school."

"Maybe," Kris replied, trying to hide how annoyed she was.

After dinner, Mr. Powell called from Portland, and they all talked with him. Lindy told him about her success with Slappy at the birthday party. Kris told him about being asked to host the concert with Mr. Wood. Her father promised he wouldn't schedule any road trips so that he could attend the concert.

After watching a video their mother had rented at the mall, the two sisters went up to their room. It was a little after eleven.

Kris clicked on the light. Lindy followed her in.

They both glanced across the room to the chair where they kept the two dummies — and gasped.

"Oh, no!" Lindy cried, raising one hand to her wide open mouth.

Earlier that night, the dummies had been placed side by side in a sitting position.

But now Slappy was upside down, falling out of the chair, his head on the floor. His brown shoes had been pulled off his feet and tossed against the wall. His suit jacket had been pulled halfway down his arms, trapping his hands behind his back.

"L-look!" Kris stammered, although her sister was already staring in horror at the scene. "Mr. Wood — he's . . ." Kris's voice caught in her throat.

Mr. Wood was sprawled on top of Slappy. His hands were wrapped around Slappy's throat, as if he were strangling him.

10

"I — I don't believe this!" Kris managed to whisper. She turned and caught the frightened expression on Lindy's face.

"What's going *on*?" Lindy cried.

Both sisters hurried across the room. Kris grabbed Mr. Wood by the back of the neck and pulled him off the other dummy. She felt as if she were separating two fighting boys.

She held Mr. Wood up in front of her, examining him carefully, staring at his face as if half-expecting him to talk to her.

Then she lowered the dummy and tossed it face-down onto her bed. Her face was pale and taut with fear.

Lindy stooped and picked up Slappy's brown shoes from the floor. She held them up and studied them, as if they would offer a clue as to what had happened.

"Kris — did you do this?" Lindy asked softly.

"Huh? Me?" Kris reacted with surprise.

"I mean, I *know* you're jealous of Slappy and me — " Lindy started.

"Whoa. Wait a minute," Kris replied angrily in a shrill, trembling voice. "I didn't do this, Lindy. Don't accuse me."

Lindy glared at her sister, studying her face. Then her expression softened and she sighed. "I don't get. I just don't get it. Look at Slappy. He's nearly been torn apart."

She set the shoes down on the chair and picked the dummy up gently as if picking up a baby. Holding him in one hand, she struggled to pull his suit jacket up with the other.

Kris heard her sister mutter something. It sounded like "Your dummy is evil."

"What did you say?" Kris demanded.

"Nothing," Lindy replied, still struggling with the jacket. "I'm . . . uh . . . I'm kind of scared about this," Lindy confessed, blushing, avoiding Kris's eyes.

"Me, too," Kris admitted. "Something weird is going on. I think we should tell Mom."

Lindy buttoned the jacket. Then she sat down on the bed with Slappy on her lap and started to replace the dummy's shoes. "Yeah. I guess we should," she replied. "It — it's just so creepy."

Their mother was in bed, reading a Stephen King novel. Her bedroom was dark except for a tiny reading lamp on her headboard that threw down a narrow triangle of yellow light.

Mrs. Powell uttered a short cry as her two daughters appeared out of the shadows. "Oh. You startled me. This is such a scary book, and I think I was just about to fall asleep."

"Can we talk to you?" Kris asked eagerly in a low whisper.

"Something weird is going on," Lindy added.

Mrs. Powell yawned and closed her book. "What's wrong?"

"It's about Mr. Wood," Kris said. "He's been doing a lot of strange things."

"Huh?" Mrs. Powell's eyes opened wide. She looked pale and tired under the harsh light from the reading lamp.

"He was strangling Slappy," Lindy reported. "And this afternoon, he said some really gross things. And — "

"Stop!" Mrs. Powell ordered, raising one hand. "Just stop."

"But, Mom — " Kris started.

"Give me a break, girls," their mother said wearily. "I'm tired of your silly competitions."

"You don't understand," Lindy interrupted.

"Yes, I *do* understand," Mrs. Powell said sharply. "You two are even competing with those ventriloquist dummies."

"Mom, please!"

"I want it to stop right now," Mrs. Powell

insisted, tossing the book onto her bed table. "I mean it. I don't want to hear another word from either of you about those dummies. If you two have problems, settle it between yourselves."

"Mom, listen — "

"And if you can't settle it, I'll take the dummies away. Both of them. I'm serious." Mrs. Powell reached above her head and clicked off the reading light, throwing the room into darkness. "Good night," she said.

The girls had no choice but to leave the room. They slunk down the hall in silence.

Kris hesitated at the doorway to their bedroom. She expected to find Mr. Wood strangling Slappy again. She breathed a sigh of relief when she saw the two dummies on the bed where they had been left.

"Mom wasn't too helpful," Lindy said dryly, rolling her eyes. She picked up Slappy and started to arrange him in the chair in front of the window.

"I think she was asleep and we woke her up," Kris replied.

She picked up Mr. Wood and started toward the chair with him — then stopped. "You know what? I think I'm going to put him in the closet tonight," she said thoughtfully.

"Good idea," Lindy said, climbing into bed.

Kris glanced down at the dummy, half-expecting him to react. To complain. To start calling her names.

But Mr. Wood grinned up at her, his painted eyes dull and lifeless.

Kris felt a chill of fear.

I'm becoming afraid of a stupid ventriloquist's dummy, she thought.

I'm shutting him up in the closet tonight because I'm afraid.

She carried Mr. Wood to the closet. Then, with a groan, she raised him high above her head and slid him onto the top shelf. Carefully closing the closet door, listening for the click, she made her way to her bed.

She slept fitfully, tossing on top of the covers, her sleep filled with disturbing dreams. She awoke to find her nightshirt completely twisted, cutting off the circulation to her right arm. She struggled to straighten it, then fell back to sleep.

She awoke early, drenched in sweat. The sky was still dawn-gray outside the window.

The room felt hot and stuffy. She sat up slowly, feeling weary, as if she hadn't slept at all.

Blinking away the sleep, her eyes focused on the chair in front of the window.

There sat Slappy, exactly where Lindy had placed him.

And beside him sat Mr. Wood, his arm around Slappy's shoulder, grinning triumphantly at Kris as if he had just pulled off a wonderful joke.

11

"Now, Mr. Wood, do you go to school?"

"Of course I do. Do you think I'm a dummy?"

"And what's your favorite class?"

"Wood shop, of course!"

"What project are you building in shop class, Mr. Wood?"

"I'm building a *girl* dummy! What else? Ha-ha! Think I want to spend the rest of my life on *your* lap?!"

Kris sat in front of the dressing table mirror with Mr. Wood on her lap, studying herself as she practiced her routine for the school concert.

Mr. Wood had been well-behaved for two days. No frightening, mysterious incidents. Kris was beginning to feel better. Maybe everything would go okay from now on.

She leaned close to the mirror, watching her lips as she made the dummy talk.

The b's and the m's were impossible to pronounce without moving her lips. She'd just have to avoid those sounds as best she could.

I'm getting better at switching from Mr. Wood's voice back to mine, she thought happily. But I've got to switch faster. The faster he and I talk, the funnier it is.

"Let's try it again, Mr. Wood," she said, pulling her chair closer to the mirror.

"Work, work, work," she made the dummy grumble.

Before she could begin the routine, Lindy came rushing breathlessly into the room. Kris watched her sister in the mirror as she came up behind her, her long hair flying loosely over her shoulders, an excited smile on her face.

"Guess what?" Lindy asked.

Kris started to reply, but Lindy didn't give her a chance.

"Mrs. Petrie was at Amy Marshall's birthday party," Lindy gushed excitedly. "She works for Channel Three. You know. The TV station. And she thinks I'm good enough to go on *Talent Search*, the show they have every week."

"Huh? Really?" was all Kris could manage in reply.

Lindy leapt excitedly in the air and cheered. "Slappy and I are going to be on TV!" she cried. "Isn't that *fabulous*?"

Staring at her sister's jubilant reflection in the mirror, Kris felt a stab of jealousy.

"I've got to tell Mom!" Lindy declared. "Hey,

Mom! Mom!" She ran from the room. Kris heard her shouting all the way down the stairs.

"Aaaaaargh!" Kris couldn't hold it in. She uttered an angry cry.

"Why does everything good happen to Lindy?" Kris screamed aloud. "I'm hosting a stupid concert for maybe a hundred parents — and she's going to be on TV! I'm just as good as she is. Maybe better!"

In a rage, she raised Mr. Wood high over her head and slammed him to the floor.

The dummy's head made a loud *clonk* as it hit the hardwood floor. The wide mouth flew open as if about to scream.

"Oh." Kris struggled to regain her composure.

Mr. Wood, crumpled at her feet, stared up at her accusingly.

Kris lifted him up and cradled the dummy against her. "There, there, Mr. Wood," she whispered soothingly. "Did I hurt you? Did I? I'm so sorry. I didn't mean to."

The dummy continued to stare up at her. His painted grin hadn't changed, but his eyes seemed cold and unforgiving.

It was a still night. No breeze. The curtains in front of the open bedroom window didn't flutter or move. Pale silver moonlight filtered in, creating long, purple shadows that appeared to creep across the girls' bedroom.

Lindy had been sleeping fitfully, a light sleep filled with busy, colorful dreams. She was startled awake by a sound. A gentle *thud*.

"Huh?" she raised her head from the damp pillow and turned.

Someone was moving in the darkness.

The sounds she'd heard were footsteps.

"Hey!" she whispered, wide awake now. "Who is it?"

The figure turned in the doorway, a shadow against even blacker shadows. "It's only me," came a whispered reply.

"Kris?"

"Yeah. Something woke me up. My throat is sore," Kris whispered from the doorway. "I'm going down to the kitchen for a glass of water."

She disappeared into the shadows. Her head still raised off the pillow, Lindy listened to her footsteps padding down the stairs.

When the sounds faded, Lindy shut her eyes and lowered her head to the pillow.

A few seconds later, she heard Kris's scream of horror.

12

Her heart pounding, Lindy struggled out of bed. The sheet tangled around her legs, and she nearly fell.

Kris's bloodcurdling scream echoed in her ears.

She practically leapt down the dark stairway, her bare feet thudding hard on the thin carpet of the steps.

It was dark downstairs, except for a thin sliver of yellow light from the kitchen.

"Kris — Kris — are you okay?" Lindy called, her voice sounding small and frightened in the dark hallway.

"Kris?"

Lindy stopped at the kitchen doorway.

What was that eerie light?

It took her a while to focus. Then she realized she was staring at the dim yellow light from inside the refrigerator.

The refrigerator door was wide open.

And . . . the refrigerator was empty.

"What — what's going on here?"

She took a step into the kitchen. Then another. Something cold and wet surrounded her foot.

Lindy gasped and, looking down, saw that she had stepped into a wide puddle.

An overturned milk carton beside her foot revealed that the puddle was spilled milk.

She raised her eyes to Kris, who was standing in darkness across the room, her back against the wall, her hands raised to her face in horror.

"Kris, what on earth — "

The scene was coming into focus now. It was all so weird, so . . . *wrong*. It was taking Lindy a long time to see the whole picture.

But, now, following Kris's horrified stare, Lindy saw the mess on the floor. And realized why the refrigerator was empty.

Everything inside it had been pulled out and dumped on the kitchen floor. An orange juice bottle lay on its side in a puddle of orange juice. Eggs were scattered everywhere. Fruits and vegetables were strewn over the floor.

"Ohh!" Lindy moaned in utter disbelief.

Everything seemed to sparkle and gleam.

What was all that shiny stuff among the food? Kris's jewelry!

There were earrings and bracelets and strands of beads tossed everywhere, mixed with the spilled, strewn food like some kind of bizarre salad.

"Oh, no!' Lindy shrieked as her eyes came to rest on the figure on the floor.

Sitting upright in the middle of the mess was Mr. Wood, grinning gleefully at her. He had several strands of beads around his neck, long, dangling earrings hanging from his ears, and a platter of leftover chicken on his lap.

13

"Kris, are you *okay*?" Lindy cried, turning her eyes away from the grinning, jewelry-covered dummy.

Kris didn't seem to hear her.

"Are you okay?" Lindy repeated the question.

"Wh-what's going on?" Kris stammered, her back pressed against the wall, her expression taut with terror. "Who — who *did* this? Did Mr. Wood — ?"

Lindy started to reply. But their mother's howl of surprise from the doorway cut off her words. "Mom — " Lindy cried, spinning around.

Mrs. Powell clicked on the ceiling light. The kitchen seemed to flare up. All three of them blinked, struggling to adjust to the sudden brightness.

"What on earth!" Mrs. Powell cried. She started

to call to her husband, then remembered he wasn't home. "I — I don't believe this!"

Barky came bounding into the room, his tail wagging. He lowered his head and started to lick up some spilled milk.

"Out you go," Mrs. Powell said sternly. She picked up the dog, carried him out, and closed the kitchen door. Then she strode into the center of the room, shaking her head, her bare feet narrowly missing the puddle of milk.

"I came down for a drink, and I — I found this mess," Kris said in a trembling voice. "The food. My jewelry. Everything . . ."

"Mr. Wood did it," Lindy accused. "Look at him!"

"*Stop it! Stop it!*" Mrs. Powell screamed. "I've had enough."

Mrs. Powell surveyed the mess, frowning and tugging at a strand of blonde hair. Her eyes stopped on Mr. Wood, and she uttered a groan of disgust.

"I knew it," she said in a low voice, raising her eyes accusingly to the two girls. "I knew this had something to do with those ventriloquist dummies."

"Mr. Wood did it, Mom," Kris said heatedly, stepping away from the wall, her hands tensed into fists. "I know it sounds dumb, but — "

"Stop it," Mrs. Powell ordered, narrowing her

eyes. "This is just sick. Sick!" She stared hard at the jewel-bedecked dummy, who grinned up at her over the big platter of chicken.

"I'm going to take the dummies away from you both," Mrs. Powell said, turning back to Lindy and Kris. "This whole thing has just gotten out of control."

"No!" Kris cried.

"That's not fair!" Lindy declared.

"I'm sorry. They have to be put away," Mrs. Powell said firmly. She let her eyes move over the cluttered floor, and let out another weary sigh. "Look at my kitchen."

"But I didn't do anything!" Lindy screamed.

"I need Mr. Wood for the spring concert!" Kris protested. "Everyone is counting on me, Mom."

Mrs. Powell glanced from one to the other. Her eyes stayed on Kris. "That's *your* dummy on the floor, right?"

"Yeah," Kris told her. "But I didn't do this. I swear!"

"You both swear you didn't do it, right?" Mrs. Powell said, suddenly looking very tired under the harsh ceiling light.

"Yes," Lindy answered quickly.

"Then you both lose your dummies. I'm sorry," Mrs. Powell said. "One of you is lying. I — I really can't believe this."

A heavy silence blanketed the room as all three Powells stared down in dismay at the mess on the floor.

Kris was the first to speak. "Mom, what if Lindy and I clean everything up?"

Lindy caught on quickly. Her face brightened. "Yeah. What if we put everything back. Right now. Make the kitchen just like normal. Make it spotless. Can we keep our dummies?"

Mrs. Powell shook her head. "No. I don't think so. Look at this mess. All the vegetables are spoiled. And the milk."

"We'll replace it all," Kris said quickly. "With our allowance. And we'll clean it up perfectly. Please. If we do that, give us one more chance?"

Mrs. Powell twisted her face in concentration, debating with herself. She stared at her daughters' eager faces. "Okay," she replied finally. "I want the kitchen spotless when I come down in the morning. All the food, all the jewelry. Everything back where it goes."

"Okay," both girls said in unison.

"And I don't want to see either of those dummies down here in my kitchen again," Mrs. Powell demanded. "If you can do that, I'll give you one more chance."

"Great!" both girls cried at once.

"And I don't want to hear any more arguments

about those dummies," Mrs. Powell continued. "No more fights. No more competing. No more blaming everything on the dummies. I don't want to hear *anything* about them. Ever."

"You won't," Kris promised, glancing at her sister.

"Thanks, Mom," Lindy said. "You go to bed. We'll clean up." She gave her mother a gentle shove toward the doorway.

"Not another word," Mrs. Powell reminded them.

"Right, Mom," the twins agreed.

Their mother disappeared toward her room. They began to clean up. Kris pulled a large garbage bag from the drawer and held it while Lindy tossed in empty cartons and spoiled food.

Kris carefully collected her jewelry and carried it upstairs.

Neither girl spoke. They worked in silence, picking up, cleaning, and mopping until the kitchen was clean. Lindy closed the refrigerator door. She yawned loudly.

Kris inspected the floor on her hands and knees, making sure it was spotless. Then she picked up Mr. Wood. He grinned back at her as if it was all a big joke.

This dummy has been nothing but trouble, Kris thought.

Nothing but trouble.

She followed Lindy out of the kitchen, clicking off the light as she left. The two girls climbed the stairs silently. Neither of them had spoken a word.

Pale moonlight filtered into their room through the open window. The air felt hot and steamy.

Kris glanced at the clock. It was a little past three in the morning.

Slappy sat slumped in the chair in front of the window, moonlight shining on his grinning face. Lindy, yawning, climbed into bed, pushed down the blanket, and pulled up the sheet. She turned her face away from her sister.

Kris lowered Mr. Wood from her shoulder. *You're nothing but trouble*, she thought angrily, holding him in front of her and staring at his grinning face.

Nothing but trouble.

Mr. Wood's wide, leering grin seemed to mock her.

A chill of fear mixed with her anger.

I'm beginning to hate this dummy, she thought.

Fear him and hate him.

Angrily, she pulled open the closet door and tossed the dummy into the closet. It fell in a crumpled heap on the closet floor.

Kris slammed the closet door shut.

Her heart thudding, she climbed into bed and pulled up the covers. She suddenly felt very tired. Her entire body ached from weariness.

She buried her face in the pillow and shut her eyes.

She had just about fallen asleep when she heard the tiny voice.

"Let me out! Let me out of here!" it cried. A muffled voice, coming from inside the closet.

14

"Let me out! Let me out!" the high-pitched voice called angrily.

Kris sat up with a jolt. Her entire body convulsed in a shudder of fear.

Her eyes darted to the other bed. Lindy hadn't moved.

"Did — did you hear it?" Kris stammered.

"Hear what?" Lindy asked sleepily.

"The voice," Kris whispered. "In the closet."

"Huh?" Lindy asked sleepily. "What are you talking about? It's three in the morning. Can't we get some sleep?"

"But, Lindy — " Kris lowered her feet to the floor. Her heart was thudding in her chest. "Wake up. Listen to me! Mr. Wood was calling to me. He was *talking*!"

Lindy raised her head and listened.

Silence.

"I don't hear anything, Kris. Really. Maybe you were dreaming."

"No!" Kris shrieked, feeling herself lose control. "It wasn't a dream! I'm so scared, Lindy. I'm just so *scared*!"

Suddenly Kris was trembling all over, and hot tears were pouring down her cheeks.

Lindy stood up and moved to the edge of her sister's bed.

"Something h-horrible is going on here, Lindy," Kris stammered through her tears.

"And I know who's doing it," Lindy whispered, leaning over her twin, putting a comforting hand on her quivering shoulder.

"Huh?"

"Yes. I know who's been doing it all," Lindy whispered. "I know who it is."

"Who?" Kris asked breathlessly.

15

"Who?" Kris repeated, letting the tears run down her cheeks. "Who?"

"*I* have," Lindy said. Her smile spread into a grin almost as wide as Slappy's. She closed her eyes and laughed.

"Huh?" Kris didn't understand. "What did you say?"

"I said I have been doing it," Lindy repeated. "Me. Lindy. It was all a joke, Kris. I gotcha again." She nodded her head as if confirming her words.

Kris gaped at her twin in disbelief. "It was all a joke?"

Lindy kept nodding.

"You moved Mr. Wood during the night? You dressed him in my clothes and made him say those gross things to me? You put him in the kitchen? You made that horrible mess?"

Lindy chuckled. "Yeah. I really scared you, didn't I?"

Kris balled her hands into angry fists. "But — but — " she sputtered. *"Why?"*

"For fun," Lindy replied, dropping back onto her bed, still grinning.

"Fun?"

"I wanted to see if I could scare you," Lindy explained. "It was just a joke. You know. I can't *believe* you fell for that voice in the closet just now! I must be a really good ventriloquist!"

"But, Lindy — "

"You really believed Mr. Wood was alive or something!" Lindy said, laughing, enjoying her victory. "You're such a nit!"

"Nit?"

"Half a nitwit!" Lindy burst into wild laughter.

"It isn't funny," Kris said softly.

"I know," Lindy replied. "It's a riot! You should've seen the look on your face when you saw Mr. Wood downstairs in your precious beads and earrings!"

"How — how did you ever *think* of such a mean joke?" Kris demanded.

"It just came to me," Lindy answered with some pride. "When you got your dummy."

"You didn't want me to get a dummy," Kris said thoughtfully.

"You're right," Lindy quickly agreed. "I wanted something that would be mine, for a change. I'm so tired of you being a copycat. So — "

"So you thought of this mean joke," Kris accused.

Lindy nodded.

Kris strode angrily to the window and pressed her forehead against the glass. "I — I can't believe I was so stupid," she muttered.

"Neither can I," Lindy agreed, grinning again.

"You really made me start thinking that Mr. Wood was alive or something," Kris said, staring out the window to the back yard below. "You really made me afraid of him."

"Aren't I brilliant!" Lindy proclaimed.

Kris turned to face her sister. "I'm never speaking to you again," she said angrily.

Lindy shrugged. "It was just a joke."

"No," Kris insisted. "It was too mean to be just a joke. I'm never speaking to you again. Never."

"Fine," Lindy replied curtly. "I thought you had a sense of humor. Fine." She slid into bed, her back to Kris, and pulled the covers up over her head.

I've got to find a way to pay her back for this, Kris thought. *But how?*

16

After school a few days later, Kris walked home with Cody. It was a hot, humid afternoon. The trees were still, and seemed to throw little shade on the sidewalk. The air above the pavement shimmered in the heat.

"Wish we had a swimming pool," Kris muttered, pulling her backpack off her shoulder.

"I wish you had one, too," Cody said, wiping his forehead with the sleeve of his red T-shirt.

"I'd like to dive into an enormous pool of iced tea," Kris said, "like in the TV commercials. It always looks so cold and refreshing."

Cody made a face. "Swim in iced tea? With ice cubes and lemon?"

"Forget it," Kris muttered.

They crossed the street. A couple of kids they knew rode by on bikes. Two men in white uniforms were up on ladders, leaning against the corner house, painting the gutters.

"Bet they're hot," Cody remarked.

"Let's change the subject," Kris suggested.

"How are you doing with Mr. Wood?" Cody asked.

"Not bad," Kris said. "I think I've got some pretty good jokes. I should be ready for the concert tomorrow night."

They stopped at the corner and let a large blue van rumble past.

"Are you talking to your sister?" Cody asked as they crossed the street. The bright sunlight made his white-blond hair glow.

"A little," Kris said, making a face. "I'm talking to her. But I haven't forgiven her."

"That was such a dumb stunt she pulled," Cody said sympathetically. He wiped the sweat off his forehead with the sleeve of his T-shirt.

"It just made me feel like such a dork," Kris admitted. "I mean, I was so stupid. She really had me believing that Mr. Wood was doing all that stuff." Kris shook her head. Thinking about it made her feel embarrassed all over again.

Her house came into view. She unzipped the back compartment of her backpack and searched for the keys.

"Did you tell your mom about Lindy's practical joke?" Cody asked.

Kris shook her head. "Mom is totally disgusted. We're not allowed to mention the dummies to her. Dad got home from Portland last night, and Mom told him what was going on. So we're not allowed to mention the dummies to him, either!" She found the keys and started up the drive. "Thanks for walking home with me."

"Yeah. Sure." Cody gave her a little wave and continued on toward his house up the street.

Kris pushed the key into the front door lock. She could hear Barky jumping and yipping excitedly on the other side of the door. "I'm coming, Barky," she called in. "Hold your horses."

She pushed open the door. Barky began leaping on her, whimpering as if she'd been away for months. "Okay, okay!" she cried laughing.

It took several minutes to calm the dog down. Then Kris got a snack from the kitchen and headed up to her room to practice with Mr. Wood.

She hoisted the dummy up from the chair where it had spent the day beside Lindy's dummy. A can of Coke in one hand, the dummy over her shoulder, she headed to the dressing table and sat down in front of the mirror.

This was the best time of day to rehearse, Kris thought. No one was home. Her parents were at work. Lindy was at some after-school activity.

She arranged Mr. Wood on her lap. "Time to go to work," she made him say, reaching into his back to move his lips. She made his eyes slide back and forth.

A button on his plaid shirt had come unbuttoned. Kris leaned him down against the dressing table and started to fasten it.

Something caught her eye. Something yellow inside the pocket.

"Weird," Kris said aloud. "I never noticed anything in there."

Slipping two fingers into the slender pocket, she pulled out a yellowed sheet of paper, folded up.

Probably just the receipt for him, Kris thought.

She unfolded the sheet of paper and held it up to read it.

It wasn't a receipt. The paper contained a single sentence handwritten very cleanly in bold black ink. It was in a language Kris didn't recognize.

"Did someone send you a love note, Mr. Wood?" she asked the dummy.

It stared up at her lifelessly.

Kris lowered her eyes to the paper and read the strange sentence out loud:

"Karru marri odonna loma molonu karrano."

What language is *that*? Kris wondered.

She glanced down at the dummy and uttered a low cry of surprise.

Mr. Wood appeared to blink.

But that wasn't possible — *was* it?

Kris took a deep breath, then let it out slowly.

The dummy stared up at her, his painted eyes as dull and wide open as ever.

Let's not get paranoid, Kris scolded herself.

"Time to work, Mr. Wood," she told him. She folded up the piece of yellow paper and slipped it back into his shirt pocket. Then she raised him to a sitting position, searching for the eye and mouth controls with her hand.

"How are things around *your* house, Mr. Wood?"

"Not good, Kris. I've got termites. I need termites like I need another hole in my head! Ha-ha!"

"Lindy! Kris! Could you come downstairs, please!" Mr. Powell called from the foot of the stairs.

It was after dinner, and the twins were up in their room. Lindy was sprawled on her stomach on the bed, reading a book for school. Kris was in front of the dressing table mirror, rehearsing quietly with Mr. Wood for tomorrow night's concert.

"What do you want, Dad?" Lindy shouted down, rolling her eyes.

"We're kind of busy," Kris shouted, shifting the dummy on her lap.

"The Millers are here, and they're dying to see your ventriloquist acts," their father shouted up.

Lindy and Kris both groaned. The Millers were the elderly couple who lived next door. They were very nice people, but very boring.

The twins heard Mr. Powell's footsteps on the stairs. A few seconds later, he poked his head into their room. "Come on, girls. Just put on a short show for the Millers. They came over for coffee, and we told them about your dummies."

"But I have to rehearse for tomorrow night," Kris insisted.

"Rehearse on them," her father suggested. "Come on. Just do five minutes. They'll get a real kick out of it."

Sighing loudly, the girls agreed. Carrying their dummies over their shoulders, they followed their father down to the living room.

Mr. and Mrs. Miller were side by side on the couch, coffee mugs in front of them on the low coffee table. They smiled and called out cheerful greetings as the girls appeared.

Kris was always struck by how much the Millers looked alike. They both had slender, pink faces topped with spongy white hair. They both wore silver-framed bifocals, which slipped down on nearly identical, pointy noses. They both had the same smile. Mr. Miller had a small, gray mustache. Lindy always joked that he grew it so the Millers could tell each other apart.

Is *that* what happens to you when you've been married a long time? Kris found herself thinking. You start to look exactly alike?

The Millers were even dressed alike, in loose-fitting tan Bermuda shorts and white cotton sports shirts.

"Lindy and Kris took up ventriloquism a few weeks ago," Mrs. Powell was explaining, twisting herself forward to see the girls from the armchair. She motioned them to the center of the room. "And they both seem to have some talent for it."

"Have you girls ever heard of Bergen and McCarthy?" Mrs. Miller asked, smiling.

"Who?" Lindy and Kris asked in unison.

"Before your time," Mr. Miller said, chuckling. "They were a ventriloquist act."

"Can you do something for us?" Mrs. Miller asked, picking up her coffee mug and setting it in her lap.

Mr. Powell pulled a dining room chair into the center of the room. "Here. Lindy, why don't you go first?" He turned to the Millers. "They're very good. You'll see," he said.

Lindy sat down and arranged Slappy on her lap. The Millers applauded. Mrs. Miller nearly spilled her coffee, but she caught the mug just in time.

"Don't applaud — just throw money!" Lindy made Slappy say. Everyone laughed as if they'd never heard that before.

Kris watched from the stairway as Lindy did a short routine. Lindy was really good, she had to admit. Very smooth. The Millers were laughing so hard, their faces were bright red. An identical shade of red. Mrs. Miller kept squeezing her husband's knee when she laughed.

Lindy finished to big applause. The Millers gushed about how wonderful she was. Lindy told them about the TV show she might be on, and they promised they wouldn't miss it. "We'll tape it," Mr. Miller said.

Kris took her place on the chair and sat Mr. Wood up in her lap. "This is Mr. Wood," she told the Millers. "We're going to be the hosts of the spring concert at school tomorrow night. So I'll give you a preview of what we're going to say."

"That's a nice-looking dummy," Mrs. Miller said quietly.

"You're a nice-looking dummy, too!" Mr. Wood declared in a harsh, raspy growl of a voice.

Kris's mother gasped. The Millers' smiles faded.

Mr. Wood leaned forward on Kris's lap and stared at Mr. Miller. *"Is that a mustache, or are you eating a rat?"* he asked nastily.

Mr. Miller glanced uncomfortably at his wife, then forced a laugh. They both laughed.

"Don't laugh so hard. You might drop your false teeth!" Mr. Wood shouted. *"And how do you get your teeth that disgusting shade of yellow? Does your bad breath do that?"*

"Kris!" Mrs. Powell shouted. "That's enough!"

The Millers' faces were bright red now, their expressions bewildered.

"That's not funny. Apologize to the Millers," Mr. Powell insisted, crossing the room and standing over Kris.

"I — I didn't say any of it!" Kris stammered. "Really, I — "

"Kris — apologize!" her father demanded angrily.

Mr. Wood turned to the Millers. *"I'm sorry,"* he rasped. *"I'm sorry you're so ugly! I'm sorry you're so old and stupid, too!"*

The Millers stared at each other unhappily. "I don't get her humor," Mrs. Miller said.

"It's just crude insults," Mr. Miller replied quietly.

"Kris — what is *wrong* with you!" Mrs. Powell demanded. She had crossed the room to stand beside her husband. "Apologize to the Millers right now! I don't *believe* you!"

"I — I — " Gripping Mr. Wood tightly around the waist, Kris rose to her feet. "I — I — " She tried to utter an apology, but no words would come out.

"Sorry!" she finally managed to scream. Then, with an embarrassed cry, she turned and fled up the stairs, tears streaming down her face.

17

"You *have* to believe me!" Kris cried in a trembling voice. "I really didn't say any of those things. Mr. Wood was talking by himself!"

Lindy rolled her eyes. "Tell me another one," she muttered sarcastically.

Lindy had followed Kris upstairs. Down in the living room, her parents were still apologizing to the Millers. Now, Kris sat on the edge of her bed, wiping tears off her cheeks. Lindy stood with her arms crossed in front of the dressing table.

"I don't make insulting jokes like that," Kris said, glancing at Mr. Wood, who lay crumpled in the center of the floor where Kris had tossed him. "You know that isn't my sense of humor."

"So why'd you do it?" Lindy demanded. "Why'd you want to make everyone mad?"

"But I *didn't*!" Kris shrieked, tugging at the sides of her hair. "Mr. Wood said those things! I didn't!"

"How can you be such a copycat?" Lindy asked

disgustedly. "I already *did* that joke, Kris. Can't you think of something original?"

"It's not a joke," Kris insisted. "Why don't you believe me?"

"No way," Lindy replied, shaking her head, her arms still crossed in front of her chest. "No way I'm going to fall for the same gag."

"Lindy, please!" Kris pleaded. "I'm frightened. I'm really frightened."

"Yeah. Sure," Lindy said sarcastically. "I'm shaking all over, too. Wow. You really fooled me, Kris. Guess you showed me you can play funny tricks, too."

"Shut up!" Kris snapped. More tears formed in the corners of her eyes.

"Very good crying," Lindy said. "But it doesn't fool me, either. And it won't fool Mom and Dad." She turned and picked up Slappy. "Maybe Slappy and I should practice some jokes. After your performance tonight, Mom and Dad might not let you do the concert tomorrow night."

She slung Slappy over her shoulder and, stepping over the crumpled form of Mr. Wood, hurried from the room.

It was hot and noisy backstage in the auditorium. Kris's throat was dry, and she kept walking over to the water fountain and slurping mouthfuls of the warm water.

The voices of the audience on the other side of

the curtain seemed to echo off all four walls and the ceiling. The louder the noise became as the auditorium filled, the more nervous Kris felt.

How am I ever going to do my act in front of all those people? she asked herself, pulling the edge of the curtain back a few inches and peering out. Her parents were off to the side, in the third row.

Seeing them brought memories of the night before flooding back to Kris. Her parents had grounded her for two weeks as punishment for insulting the Millers. They almost hadn't let her come to the concert.

Kris stared at the kids and adults filing into the large auditorium, recognizing a lot of faces. She realized her hands were ice cold. Her throat was dry again.

Don't think of it as an audience, she told herself. Think of it as a bunch of kids and parents, most of whom you know.

Somehow that made it worse.

She let go of the curtain, hurried to get one last drink from the fountain, then retrieved Mr. Wood from the table she had left him on.

It suddenly grew quiet on the other side of the curtain. The concert was about to begin.

"Break a leg!" Lindy called across to her as she hurried to join the other chorus members.

"Thanks," Kris replied weakly. She pulled up

Mr. Wood and straightened his shirt. "Your hands are clammy!" she made him say.

"No insults tonight," Kris told him sternly.

To her shock, the dummy blinked.

"Hey!" she cried. She hadn't touched his eye controls.

She had a stab of fear that went beyond stage fright. Maybe I shouldn't go on with this, she thought, staring intently at Mr. Wood, watching for him to blink again.

Maybe I should say I'm sick and not perform with him.

"Are you nervous?" a voice whispered.

"Huh?" At first, she thought it was Mr. Wood. But then she quickly realized that it was Mrs. Berman, the music teacher.

"Yeah. A little," Kris admitted, feeling her face grow hot.

"You'll be terrific," Mrs. Berman gushed, squeezing Kris's shoulder with a sweaty hand. She was a large, heavyset woman with several chins, a red lipsticked mouth, and flowing black hair. She was wearing a long, loose-fitting dress of red-and-blue flower patterns. "Here goes," she said, giving Kris's shoulder one more squeeze.

Then she stepped onstage, blinking against the harsh white light of the spotlight, to introduce Kris and Mr. Wood.

Am I really doing this? Kris asked herself.

Can I do this?

Her heart was pounding so hard, she couldn't hear Mrs. Berman's introduction. Then, suddenly, the audience was applauding, and Kris found herself walking across the stage to the microphone, carrying Mr. Wood in both hands.

Mrs. Berman, her flowery dress flowing around her, was heading offstage. She smiled at Kris and gave her an encouraging wink as they passed each other.

Squinting against the bright spotlight, Kris walked to the middle of the stage. Her mouth felt as dry as cotton. She wondered if she could make a sound.

A folding chair had been set up for her. She sat down, arranging Mr. Wood on her lap, then realized that the microphone was much too high.

This drew titters of soft laughter from the audience.

Embarrassed, Kris stood up and, holding Mr. Wood under one arm, struggled to lower the microphone.

"Are you having trouble?" Mrs. Berman called from the side of the stage. She hurried over to help Kris.

But before the music teacher got halfway across the stage, Mr. Wood leaned into the microphone. *"What time does the blimp go up?"* he rasped nastily, staring at Mrs. Berman's dress.

"What?" She stopped in surprise.

"Your face reminds me of a wart I had removed!" Mr. Wood growled at the startled woman.

Her mouth dropped open in horror. "Kris!"

"If we count your chins, will it tell us your age?"

There was laughter floating up from the audience. But it was mixed with gasps of horror.

"Kris — that's enough!" Mrs. Berman cried, the microphone picking up her angry protest.

"You're more than enough! You're enough for two!" Mr. Wood declared nastily. *"If you got any bigger, you'd need your own zip code!"*

"Kris — really! I'm going to ask you to apologize," Mrs. Berman said, her face bright red.

"Mrs. Berman, I — I'm not doing it!" Kris stammered. "I'm not saying these things!"

"Please apologize. To me and to the audience," Mrs. Berman demanded.

Mr. Wood leaned into the microphone. *"Apologize for THIS!"* he screamed.

The dummy's head tilted back. His jaw dropped. His mouth opened wide.

And a thick green liquid came spewing out.

"Yuck!" someone screamed.

It looked like pea soup. It spurted up out of Mr. Wood's open mouth like water rushing from a fire hose.

Voices screamed and cried out their surprise as the thick, green liquid showered over the people in the front rows.

"Stop it!"

"Help!"

"Somebody — turn it off!"

"It stinks!"

Kris froze in horror, staring as more and more of the disgusting substance poured from her dummy's gaping mouth.

A putrid stench — the smell of sour milk, of rotten eggs, of burning rubber, of decayed meat — rose up from the liquid. It puddled over the stage and showered over the front seats.

Blinded by the spotlight, Kris couldn't see the audience in front of her. But she could hear the choking and the gagging, the frantic cries for help.

"Clear the auditorium! Clear the auditorium!" Mrs. Berman was shouting.

Kris heard the rumble and scrape of people shoving their way up the aisles and out the doors.

"It stinks!"

"I'm sick!"

"Somebody — help!"

Kris tried to clamp her hand over the dummy's mouth. But the force of the putrid green liquid frothing and spewing out was too strong. It pushed her hand away.

Suddenly she realized she was being shoved from behind. Off the stage. Away from the shouting people fleeing the auditorium. Out of the glaring spotlight.

She was backstage before she realized that it was Mrs. Berman who was pushing her.

"I — I don't know how you did that. Or why!" Mrs. Berman shouted angrily, frantically wiping splotches of the disgusting green liquid off the front of her dress with both hands. "But I'm going to see that you're suspended from school, Kris! And if I have my way," she sputtered, "you'll be suspended for *life*!"

18

"That's right. Close the door," Mr. Powell said sternly, glaring with narrowed eyes at Kris.

He stood a few inches behind her, arms crossed in front of him, making sure she followed his instructions. She had carefully folded Mr. Wood in half and shoved him to the back of her closet shelf. Now she closed the closet, making sure it was completely shut, as he ordered.

Lindy watched silently from her bed, her expression troubled.

"Does the closet door lock?" Mr. Powell asked.

"No. Not really," Kris told him, lowering her head.

"Well, that will have to do," he said. "On Monday, I'm taking him back to the pawn shop. Do not take him out until then."

"But, Dad —"

He raised a hand to silence her.

"We have to talk about this," Kris pleaded. "You have to listen to me. What happened tonight — it wasn't a practical joke. I — "

Her father turned away from her, a scowl on his face. "Kris, I'm sorry. We'll talk tomorrow. Your mother and I — we're both too angry and too upset to talk now."

"But, Dad — "

Ignoring her, he stormed out of the room. She listened to his footsteps, hard and hurried, down the stairs. Then Kris slowly turned to Lindy. "Now do you believe me?"

"I — I don't know what to believe," Lindy replied. "It was just so . . . unbelievably gross."

"Lindy, I — I — "

"Daddy's right. Let's talk tomorrow," Lindy said. "I'm sure everything will be clearer and calmer tomorrow."

But Kris couldn't sleep. She shifted from side to side, uncomfortable, wide awake. She pulled the pillow over her face, held it there for a while, welcoming the soft darkness, then tossed it to the floor.

I'm never going to sleep again, she thought.

Every time she closed her eyes, she saw the hideous scene in the auditorium once again. She heard the astonished cries of the audience, the kids and their parents. And she heard the cries of shock turn to groans of disgust as the putrid gunk poured out over everyone.

Sickening. So totally sickening.

And everyone blamed her.

My life is ruined, Kris thought. I can never go back there again. I can never go to school. I can never show my face *anywhere*.

Ruined. My whole life. Ruined by that stupid dummy.

In the next bed, Lindy snored softly, in a slow, steady rhythm.

Kris turned her eyes to the bedroom window. The curtains hung down over the window, filtering the pale moonlight from outside. Slappy sat in his usual place in the chair in front of the window, bent in two, his head between his knees.

Stupid dummies, Kris thought bitterly. So stupid.

And now my life is ruined.

She glanced at the clock. One-twenty. Outside the window, she heard a low, rumbling sound. A soft whistle of brakes. Probably a large truck going by.

Kris yawned. She closed her eyes and saw the gross green gunk spewing out of Mr. Wood's mouth.

Will I see that every time I close my eyes? she wondered.

What on earth *was* it? How could everyone blame *me* for something so . . . so . . .

The rumbling of the truck faded into the distance.

But then Kris heard another sound. A rustling sound.

A soft footstep.

Someone was moving.

She sucked in her breath and held it, listening hard.

Silence now. Silence so heavy, she could hear the loud thudding of her heart.

Then another soft footstep.

A shadow moved.

The closet door swung open.

Or was it just shadows shifting?

No. Someone was moving. Moving from the open closet. Someone was creeping toward the bedroom door. Creeping so softly, so silently.

Her heart pounding, Kris pulled herself up, trying not to make a sound. Realizing that she'd been holding her breath, she let it out slowly, silently. She took another breath, then sat up.

The shadow moved slowly to the door.

Kris lowered her feet to the floor, staring hard into the darkness, her eyes staying with the silent, moving figure.

What's happening? she wondered.

The shadow moved again. She heard a scraping sound, the sound of a sleeve brushing the doorframe.

Kris pushed herself to her feet. Her legs felt shaky as she crept to the door, following the moving shadow.

Out into the hallway. Even darker out here because there were no windows.

Toward the stairway.

The shadow moved more quickly now.

Kris followed, her bare feet moving lightly over the thin carpet.

What's happening? What's happening?

She caught up to the shadowy figure on the landing. "Hey!" she called, her voice a tight whisper.

She grabbed the shoulder and turned the figure around.

And stared into the grinning face of Mr. Wood.

19

Mr. Wood blinked, then hissed at her, an ugly sound, a menacing sound. In the darkness of the stairwell, his painted grin became a threatening leer.

In her fright, Kris squeezed the dummy's shoulder, wrapping her fingers around the harsh fabric of his shirt.

"This — this is impossible!" she whispered.

He blinked again. He giggled. His mouth opened, making his grin grow wider.

He tried to tug out of Kris's grasp, but she hung on without even realizing she was holding him.

"But — you're a *dummy*!" she squealed.

He giggled again. "So are you," he replied. His voice was a deep growl, like the angry snarl of a large dog.

"You can't walk!" Kris cried, her voice trembling.

The dummy giggled its ugly giggle again.

"You can't be alive!" Kris exclaimed.

"Let go of me — *now!*" the dummy growled.

Kris held on, tightening her grip. "I'm dreaming," Kris told herself aloud. "I have to be dreaming."

"I'm not a dream. I'm a nightmare!" the dummy exclaimed, and tossed back his wooden head, laughing.

Still gripping the shoulder of the shirt, Kris stared through the darkness at the grinning face. The air seemed to grow heavy and hot. She felt as if she couldn't breathe, as if she were suffocating.

What was that sound?

It took her a while to recognize the strained gasps of her own breathing.

"Let go of me," the dummy repeated. "Or I'll throw you down the stairs." He tried once again to tug out of her grasp.

"No!" Kris insisted, holding tight. "I — I'm putting you back in the closet."

The dummy laughed, then pushed his painted face close to Kris's face. "You can't keep me there."

"I'm locking you in. I'm locking you in a box. In *something!*" Kris declared, panic clouding her thoughts.

The darkness seemed to descend over her, choking her, weighing her down.

"Let go of me." The dummy pulled hard.

Kris reached out her other hand and grabbed him around the waist.

"Let go of me," he snarled in his raspy, deep rumble of a voice. "I'm in charge now. You will listen to me. This is *my* house now."

He pulled hard.

Kris encircled his waist.

They both fell onto the stairs, rolling down a few steps.

"Let go!" the dummy ordered. He rolled on top of her, his wild eyes glaring into hers.

She pushed him off, tried to pin his arms behind his back.

He was surprisingly strong. He pulled back one arm, then shoved a fist hard into the pit of her stomach.

"Ohhh." Kris groaned, feeling the breath knocked out of her.

The dummy took advantage of her momentary weakness, and pulled free. Grasping the banister with one hand, he tried to pull himself past her and down the stairs.

But Kris shot out a foot and tripped him.

Still struggling to breathe, she pounced onto his back. Then she pulled him away from the banister and pushed him down hard onto a step.

"Oh!" Kris gasped loudly as the overhead hall light flashed on. She closed her eyes against the sudden harsh intrusion. The dummy struggled to pull out from under her, but she pushed down on his back with all her weight.

"Kris — what on earth — ?!" Lindy's startled voice called down from the top step.

"It's Mr. Wood!" Kris managed to cry up to her. "He's . . . *alive!*" She pushed down hard, sprawled over the dummy, keeping him pinned beneath her.

"Kris — what are you doing?" Lindy demanded. "Are you okay?"

"No!" Kris exclaimed. "I'm not okay! Please — Lindy! Go get Mom and Dad! Mr. Wood — he's alive!"

"It's just a dummy!" Lindy called down, taking a few reluctant steps toward her sister. "Get up, Kris! Have you lost your mind?"

"*Listen to me!*" Kris shrieked at the top of her lungs. "Get Mom and Dad! Before he escapes!"

But Lindy didn't move. She stared down at her sister, her long hair falling in tangles about her face, her features twisted in horror. "Get up, Kris," she urged. "Please — get up. Let's go back to bed."

"I'm *telling* you, he's *alive!*" Kris cried desperately. "You've got to believe me, Lindy. You've *got* to!"

The dummy lay lifelessly beneath her, his face buried in the carpet, his arms and legs sprawled out to the sides.

"You had a nightmare," Lindy insisted, climbing down step by step, holding her long nightshirt up above her ankles until she was standing right above Kris. "Come back to bed, Kris. It was just a nightmare. The horrible thing that happened at the concert — it gave you a nightmare, that's all."

Gasping for breath, Kris lifted herself up and twisted her head to face her sister. Grabbing the banister with one hand, she raised herself a little.

The instant she lightened up on him, the dummy grabbed the edge of the stair with both hands and pulled himself out from under her. Half-falling, half-crawling, he scrambled down the rest of the stairs.

"No! No! I don't *believe* it!" Lindy shrieked, seeing the dummy move.

"Go get Mom and Dad!" Kris said. "Hurry!"

Her mouth wide open in shocked disbelief, Lindy turned and headed back up the stairs, screaming for her parents.

Kris dived off the step, thrusting her arms in front of her.

She tackled Mr. Wood from behind, wrapping her arms around his waist.

His head hit the carpet hard as they both crumpled to the floor.

He uttered a low, throaty cry of pain. His eyes closed. He didn't move.

Dazed, her chest heaving, her entire body trembling, Kris slowly climbed to her feet. She quickly pressed a foot on the dummy's back to hold him in place.

"Mom and Dad — where *are* you?" she cried aloud. "Hurry."

The dummy raised its head. He let out an angry growl and started to thrash his arms and legs wildly.

Kris pressed her foot hard against his back.

"Let go!" he growled viciously.

Kris heard voices upstairs.

"Mom? Dad? Down here!" she called up to them.

Both of her parents appeared at the upstairs landing, their faces filled with worry.

"Look!" Kris cried, frantically pointing down to the dummy beneath her foot.

20

"Look at *what*?" Mr. Powell cried, adjusting his pajama top.

Kris pointed down to the dummy under her foot. "He — he's trying to get away," she stammered.

But Mr. Wood lay lifeless on his stomach.

"Is this supposed to be a joke?" Mrs. Powell demanded angrily, hands at the waist of her cotton nightgown.

"I don't get it," Mr. Powell said, shaking his head.

"Mr. Wood — he ran down the stairs," Kris said frantically. "He's been doing everything. He — "

"This isn't funny," Mrs. Powell said wearily, running a hand back through her blonde hair. "It isn't funny at all, Kris. Waking everyone up in the middle of the night."

"I really think you've lost your mind. I'm very worried about you," Mr. Powell added. "I mean, after what happened at school tonight — "

"Listen to me!" Kris shrieked. She bent down and pulled Mr. Wood up from the floor. Holding him by the shoulders, she shook him hard. "He moves! He runs! He talks! He — he's *alive!*"

She stopped shaking the dummy and let go. He slumped lifelessly to the floor, falling in an unmoving heap at her feet.

"I think maybe you need to see a doctor," Mr. Powell said, his face tightening with concern.

"No. I *saw* him, too!" Lindy said, coming to Kris's aid. "Kris is right. The dummy *did* move." But then she added, "I mean, I *think* it moved!"

You're a big help, Lindy, Kris thought, suddenly feeling weak, drained.

"Is this just another stupid prank?" Mrs. Powell asked angrily. "After what happened at school tonight, I'd think that would be enough."

"But, Mom — " Kris started, staring down at the lifeless heap at her feet.

"Back to bed," Mrs. Powell ordered. "There's no school tomorrow. We'll have plenty of time to discuss punishments for you two."

"*Me?*" Lindy cried, outraged. "What did *I* do?"

"Mom, we're telling the truth!" Kris insisted.

"I still don't get the joke," Mr. Powell said, shaking his head. He turned to his wife. "Were we supposed to believe her or something?"

"Get to bed. Both of you. Now!" their mother snapped. She and their father disappeared from

108

the upstairs landing, heading angrily back down the hall to their room.

Lindy remained, one hand on the top of the banister, staring down regretfully at Kris.

"You believe me, don't you?" Kris called up to her.

"Yeah. I guess," Lindy replied doubtfully, lowering her eyes to the dummy at Kris's feet.

Kris looked down, too. She saw Mr. Wood blink. He started to straighten up.

"Whoa!" She uttered an alarmed cry and grabbed him by the neck. "Lindy — hurry!" she called. "He's moving again!"

"Wh-what should we do?" Lindy stammered, making her way hesitantly down the stairs.

"I don't know," Kris replied as the dummy thrashed his arms and legs against the carpet, trying desperately to free himself from her two-handed grip on his neck. "We've got to — "

"There's *nothing* you can do," Mr. Wood snarled. "You will be my slaves now. I'm alive once again! Alive!"

"But — how?" Kris demanded, staring at him in disbelief. "I mean, you're a dummy. How — ?"

The dummy snickered. "*You* brought me back to life," he told her in his raspy voice. "You read the ancient words."

The ancient words? What was he talking about?

And then Kris remembered. She had read the

strange-sounding words from the sheet of paper in the dummy's shirt pocket.

"I am back, thanks to you," the dummy growled. "And now you and your sister will serve me."

As she stared in horror at the grinning dummy, an idea popped into Kris's mind.

The paper. She had tucked it back into his pocket.

If I read the words again, Kris thought, it will put him back to sleep.

She reached out and grabbed him. He tried to jerk away, but she was too quick.

The folded sheet of yellow paper was in her hand.

"Give me that!" he cried. He swiped at it, but Kris swung it out of his reach.

She unfolded it quickly. And before the dummy could grab the paper out of her hands, she read the strange words aloud:

"Karru marri odonna loma molonu karrano."

21

Both sisters stared at the dummy, waiting for him to collapse.

But he gripped the banister and tossed his head back in an amused, scornful laugh. "Those are the words of the ancient sorcerer to bring me to life!" he proclaimed. "Those aren't the words to kill me!"

Kill him?

Yes, Kris thought frantically. She tossed down the yellow paper disgustedly.

We have no choice.

"We have to kill him, Lindy."

"Huh?" Her sister's face filled with surprise.

Kris grabbed the dummy by the shoulders and held on tightly. "I'll hold him. You pull his head off."

Lindy was beside her now. She had to duck away from Mr. Wood's thrashing feet.

"I'll hold him still," Kris repeated. "Grab his head. Pull it off."

111

"You — you're sure?" Lindy hesitated, her features tight with fear.

"*Just do it!*" Kris screamed.

She let her hands slide down around Mr. Wood's waist.

Lindy grabbed his head in both hands.

"*Let go of me!*" the dummy rasped.

"Pull!" Kris cried to her terrified sister.

Holding the dummy tightly around the waist, she leaned back, pulling him away from her sister.

Lindy's hands were wrapped tightly around the dummy's head. With a loud groan, she pulled hard.

The head didn't come off.

Mr. Wood uttered a high-pitched giggle. "Stop. You're tickling me!" he rasped.

"Pull harder!" Kris ordered her sister.

Lindy's face was bright red. She tightened her grip on the head and pulled again, tugging with all her strength.

The dummy giggled his shrill, unpleasant giggle.

"It — it won't come off," Lindy said, sighing in defeat.

"Twist it off!" Kris suggested frantically.

The dummy thrashed out with his feet, kicking Kris in the stomach. But she held on. "Twist the head off!" she cried.

Lindy tried to turn the head.

The dummy giggled.

"It won't twist!" Lindy cried in frustration. She let go of the head and took a step back.

Mr. Wood raised his head, stared up at Lindy, and grinned. "You can't kill me. I have powers."

"What do we do?" Lindy cried, raising her eyes to Kris.

"This is my house now," the dummy rasped, grinning at Lindy as it struggled to wriggle out of Kris's arms. "You will do as I say now. Put me down."

"What do we *do*?" Lindy repeated.

"Take him upstairs. We'll *cut* his head off," Kris replied.

Mr. Wood swung his head around, his eyes stretched open in an evil glare.

"Ow!" Kris cried out in surprise as the dummy snapped his jaws over her arm, biting her. She pulled her arm away and, without thinking, slapped the dummy's wooden head with the palm of her hand.

The dummy giggled in response. "Violence! Violence!" he said in a mock scolding tone.

"Get those sharp scissors. In your drawer," Kris instructed her sister. "I'll carry him up to our room."

Her arm throbbed where he had bitten her. But she held onto him tightly and carried him up to their bedroom.

Lindy had already pulled the long metal scissors from the drawer. Her hand trembled as she opened and closed the blades.

"Below the neck," Kris said, holding Mr. Wood tightly by the shoulders.

He hissed furiously at her. She dodged as he tried to kick her with both sneakered feet.

Holding the scissors with two hands, Lindy tried cutting the head off at the neck. The scissors didn't cut, so she tried a sawing motion.

Mr. Wood giggled. "I told you. You can't kill me."

"It isn't going to work," Lindy cried, tears of frustration running down her cheeks. "Now what?"

"We'll put him in the closet. Then we can think," Kris replied.

"You have no need to think. You are my slaves," the dummy rasped. "You will do whatever I ask. I will be in charge from now on."

"No way," Kris muttered, shaking her head.

"What if we *won't* help you?" Lindy demanded.

The dummy turned to her, casting her a hard, angry stare. "Then I'll start hurting the ones you love," he said casually. "Your parents. Your friends. Or maybe that disgusting dog that's always yapping at me." He tossed back his head and a dry, evil laugh escaped his wooden lips.

"Lock him in the closet," Lindy suggested. "Till we figure out how to get rid of him."

"You *can't* get rid of me," Mr. Wood insisted. "Don't make me angry. I have powers. I'm warning you. I'm starting to get tired of your stupid attempts to harm me."

"The closet doesn't lock — remember?" Kris cried, struggling to hold onto the wriggling dummy.

"Oh. Wait. How about this?" Lindy hurried to the closet. She pulled out an old suitcase from the back.

"Perfect," Kris said.

"I'm warning you — " Mr. Wood threatened. "You are becoming very tiresome."

With a hard tug, he pulled himself free of Kris.

She dove to tackle him, but he darted out from under her. She fell facedown onto her bed.

The dummy ran to the center of the room, then turned his eyes to the doorway, as if trying to decide where to go. "You must do as I tell you," he said darkly, raising a wooden hand toward Lindy. "I will not run from you two. You are to be my slaves."

"No!" Kris cried, pushing herself up.

She and her sister both dove at the dummy. Lindy grabbed his arms. Kris ducked to grab his ankles.

Working together, they stuffed him into the open suitcase.

"You will regret this," he threatened, kicking his legs, struggling to hit them. "You will pay dearly for this. Now someone will die!"

He continued screaming after Kris latched the suitcase and shoved it into the closet. She quickly closed the closet door, then leaned her back against it, sighing wearily.

"Now what?" she asked Lindy.

22

"We'll bury him," Kris said.

"Huh?" Lindy stifled a yawn.

They had been whispering together for what seemed like hours. As they tried to come up with a plan, they could hear the dummy's muffled cries from inside the closet.

"We'll bury him. Under that huge mound of dirt," Kris explained, her eyes going to the window. "You know. Next door, at the side of the new house."

"Yeah. Okay. I don't know," Lindy replied. "I'm so tired, I can't think straight." She glanced at the bed table clock. It was nearly three-thirty in the morning. "I still think we should wake up Mom and Dad," Lindy said, fear reflected in her eyes.

"We can't," Kris told her. "We've been over that a hundred times. They won't believe us. If we wake them up, we'll be in even bigger trouble."

"How could we be in *bigger* trouble?" Lindy demanded, gesturing with her head to the closet where Mr. Wood's angry cries could still be heard.

"Get dressed," Kris said with renewed energy. "We'll bury him under all that dirt. Then we'll never have to think about him again."

Lindy shuddered and turned her eyes to her dummy, folded up in the chair. "I can't bear to look at Slappy anymore. I'm so sorry I got us interested in dummies."

"Ssshhh. Just get dressed," Kris said impatiently.

A few minutes later, the two girls crept down the stairs in the darkness. Kris carried the suitcase in both arms, trying to muffle the sound of Mr. Wood's angry protests.

They stopped at the bottom of the stairs and listened for any sign that they had awakened their parents.

Silence.

Lindy pulled open the front door and they slipped outside.

The air was surprisingly cool and wet. A heavy dew had begun to fall, making the front lawn glisten under the light of a half-moon. Blades of wet grass clung to their sneakers as they made their way to the garage.

As Kris held onto the suitcase, Lindy slowly, quietly, pulled open the garage door. When it was halfway up, she ducked and slipped inside.

A few seconds later she emerged, carrying a large snow shovel. "This should do it," she said, whispering even though no one was around.

Kris glanced down the street as they headed across the yard to the lot next door. The heavy morning dew misted the glow of the streetlamps, making the pale light appear to bend and flicker like candles. Everything seemed to shimmer under the dark purple sky.

Kris set the suitcase down beside the tall mound of dirt. "We'll dig right down here," she said, pointing toward the bottom of the mound. "We'll shove him in and cover him."

"I'm warning you," Mr. Wood threatened, listening inside the suitcase. "Your plan won't work. I have powers!"

"You dig first," Kris told her sister, ignoring the dummy's threat. "Then I'll take a turn."

Lindy dug into the pile and heaved up a shovelful of dirt. Kris shivered. The heavy dew felt cold and damp. A cloud floated over the moon, darkening the sky from purple to black.

"Let me out!" Mr. Wood called. "Let me out now, and your punishment won't be too severe."

"Dig faster," Kris whispered impatiently.

"I'm going as fast as I can," Lindy replied. She had dug a pretty good-sized square-shaped hole at the base of the mound. "How much deeper, do you think?"

"Deeper," Kris said. "Here. Watch the suitcase. I'll take a turn." She changed places with Lindy and started to dig.

Something scampered heavily near the low shrubs that separated the yards. Kris looked up, saw a moving shadow, and gasped.

"Raccoon, I think," Lindy said with a shudder. "Are we going to bury Mr. Wood in the suitcase, or are we going to take him out?"

"Think Mom will notice the suitcase is gone?" Kris asked, tossing a shovelful of wet dirt to the side.

Lindy shook her head. "We never use it."

"We'll bury him in the suitcase," Kris said. "It'll be easier."

"You'll be sorry," the dummy rasped. The suitcase shook and nearly toppled onto its side.

"I'm so sleepy," Lindy moaned, tossing her socks onto the floor, then sliding her feet under the covers.

"I'm wide awake," Kris replied, sitting on the edge of her bed. "I guess it's because I'm so happy. So happy we got rid of that awful creature."

"It's all so weird," Lindy said, adjusting her pillow behind her head. "I don't blame Mom or Dad for not believing it. I'm not sure I believe it, either."

"You put the shovel back where you found it?" Kris asked.

Lindy nodded. "Yeah," she said sleepily.

"And you closed the garage door?"

"Ssshhh. I'm asleep," Lindy said. "At least there's no school tomorrow. We can sleep late."

"I hope I can fall asleep," Kris said doubtfully. "I'm just so *pumped*. It's all like some kind of hideously gross nightmare. I just think . . . Lindy? Lindy — are you still awake?"

No. Her sister had fallen asleep.

Kris stared up at the ceiling. She pulled the blankets up to her chin. She still felt chilled. She couldn't shake the cold dampness of the early morning air.

After a short while, with thoughts of everything that had happened that night whirring crazily in her head, Kris fell asleep, too.

The rumble of machines woke her up at eight-thirty the next morning. Stretching, trying to rub the sleep from her eyes, Kris stumbled to the window, leaned over the chair holding Slappy, and peered out.

It was a gray, cloudy day. Two enormous yellow steamrollers were rolling over the lot next door behind the newly constructed house, flattening the land.

I wonder if they're going to flatten that big mound of dirt, Kris thought, staring down at them. That would really be *excellent*.

Kris smiled. She hadn't slept very long, but she felt refreshed.

Lindy was still sound asleep. Kris tiptoed past her, pulled her robe on, and headed downstairs.

"Morning, Mom," she called brightly, tying the belt to her robe as she entered the kitchen.

Mrs. Powell turned from the sink to face her. Kris was surprised to see an angry expression on her face.

She followed her mother's stare to the breakfast counter.

"Oh!" Kris gasped when she saw Mr. Wood. He was seated at the counter, his hands in his lap. His hair was matted with red-brown dirt, and he had dirt smears on his cheeks and forehead.

Kris raised her hands to her face in horror.

"I thought you were told never to bring that thing down here!" Mrs. Powell scolded. "What do I have to do, Kris?" She turned angrily back to the sink.

The dummy winked at Kris and flashed her a wide, evil grin.

23

As Kris stared in horror at the grinning dummy, Mr. Powell suddenly appeared in the kitchen doorway. "Ready?" he asked his wife.

Mrs. Powell hung the dishtowel on the rack and turned around, brushing a lock of hair off her forehead. "Ready. I'll get my bag." She brushed past him into the front hallway.

"Where are you going?" Kris cried, her voice revealing her alarm. She kept her eyes on the dummy at the counter.

"Just doing a little shopping at the garden store," her father told her, stepping into the room, peering out the kitchen window. "Looks like rain."

"Don't go!" Kris pleaded.

"Huh?" He turned toward her.

"Don't go — please!" Kris cried.

Her father's eyes landed on the dummy. He walked over to him. "Hey — what's the big idea?" her father asked angrily.

"I thought you wanted to take him back to the

pawn shop," Kris replied, thinking quickly.

"Not till Monday," her father replied. "Today is Saturday, remember?"

The dummy blinked. Mr. Powell didn't notice.

"Do you have to go shopping now?" Kris asked in a tiny voice.

Before her father could answer, Mrs. Powell reappeared in the doorway. "Here. Catch," she called, and tossed the car keys to him. "Let's go before it pours."

Mr. Powell started to the door. "Why don't you want us to go?" he asked.

"The dummy — " Kris started. But she knew it was hopeless. They'd never listen. They'd never believe her. "Never mind," she muttered.

A few seconds later, she heard their car back down the driveway. They were gone.

And she was alone in the kitchen with the grinning dummy.

Mr. Wood turned toward her slowly, swiveling the tall counter stool. His big eyes locked angrily on Kris's.

"I warned you," he rasped.

Barky came trotting into the kitchen, his toenails clicking loudly on the linoleum. He sniffed the floor as he ran, searching for breakfast scraps someone might have dropped.

"Barky, where've you been?" Kris asked, glad to have company.

The dog ignored her and sniffed under the stool Mr. Wood sat on.

"He was upstairs, waking me up," Lindy said, rubbing her eyes as she walked into the kitchen. She was wearing white tennis shorts and a sleeveless magenta T-shirt. "Stupid dog."

Barky licked at a spot on the linoleum.

Lindy cried out as she spotted Mr. Wood. "Oh, no!"

"I'm back," the dummy rasped. "And I'm very unhappy with you two slaves."

Lindy turned to Kris, her mouth open in surprise and terror.

Kris kept her eyes trained on the dummy. *What does he plan to do?* she wondered. *How can I stop him?*

Burying him under all that dirt hadn't kept him from returning. Somehow he had freed himself from the suitcase and pulled himself out.

Wasn't there any way to defeat him? Any way at all?

Grinning his evil grin, Mr. Wood dropped down to the floor, his sneakers thudding hard on the floor. "I'm very unhappy with you two slaves," he repeated in his growly voice.

"What are you going to do?" Lindy cried in a shrill, frightened voice.

"I have to punish you," the dummy replied. "I have to prove to you that I am serious."

"Wait!" Kris cried.

But the dummy moved quickly. He reached down and grabbed Barky by the neck with both hands.

As the dummy tightened his grip, the frightened terrier began to howl in pain.

24

"I warned you," Mr. Wood snarled over the howls of the little black terrier. "You will do as I say — or one by one, those you love will suffer!"

"No!" Kris cried.

Barky let out a high-pitched *whelp*, a bleat of pain that made Kris shudder.

"Let go of Barky!" Kris screamed.

The dummy giggled.

Barky uttered a hoarse gasp.

Kris couldn't stand it any longer. She and Lindy leapt at the dummy from two sides. Lindy tackled his legs. Kris grabbed Barky and tugged.

Lindy dragged the dummy to the floor. But his wooden hands held a tight grip on the dog's throat.

Barky's howls became a muffled whimper as he struggled to breathe.

"Let go! Let *go*!" Kris shrieked.

"I *warned* you!" the dummy snarled as Lindy held tight to his kicking legs. "The dog must die now!"

"No!" Kris let go of the gasping dog. She slid her hands down to the dummy's wrists. Then with a fierce tug, she pulled the wooden hands apart.

Barky dropped to the floor, wheezing. He scampered to the corner, his paws sliding frantically over the smooth floor.

"You'll pay now!" Mr. Wood growled. Jerking free from Kris, he swung his wooden hand up, landing a hard blow on Kris's forehead.

She cried out in pain and raised her hands to her head.

She heard Barky yipping loudly behind her.

"Let go of me!" Mr. Wood demanded, turning back to Lindy, who still held onto his legs.

"No way!" Lindy cried. "Kris — grab his arms again."

Her head still throbbing, Kris lunged forward to grab the dummy's arms.

But he lowered his head as she approached and clamped his wooden jaws around her wrist.

"Owww!" Kris howled in pain and pulled back.

Lindy lifted the dummy up by the legs, then slammed his body hard against the floor. He uttered a furious growl and tried to kick free of her.

Kris lunged again, and this time grabbed one arm, then the other. He lowered his head to bite once more, but she dodged away and pulled his arms tight behind his back.

"I'm warning you!" he bellowed. "I'm warning you!"

Barky yipped excitedly, hopping up on Kris.

"What do we *do* with him?" Lindy cried, shouting over the dummy's angry threats.

"Outside!" Kris yelled, pressing the arms more tightly behind Mr. Wood's back.

She suddenly remembered the two steamrollers she had seen moving over the yard next door, flattening the ground. "Come on," she urged her sister. "We'll crush him!"

"I'm warning you! I have powers!" the dummy screamed.

Ignoring him, Kris pulled open the kitchen door and they carried their wriggling captive outside.

The sky was charcoal-gray. A light rain had begun to fall. The grass was already wet.

Over the low shrubs that separated the yards, the girls could see the two enormous yellow steamrollers, one in the back, one at the side of the next-door lot. They looked like huge, lumbering animals, their giant black rollers flattening everything in their path.

"This way! Hurry!" Kris shouted to her sister, holding the dummy tightly as she ran. "Toss him under that one!"

"Let me go! Let me go, slaves!" the dummy screamed. "This is your last chance!" He swung his head hard, trying to bite Kris's arm.

Thunder rumbled, low in the distance.

The girls ran at full speed, slipping on the wet

grass as they hurried toward the fast-moving steamroller.

They were just a few yards away from the enormous machine when they saw Barky. His tail wagging furiously, he scampered ahead of them.

"Oh, no! How'd he get out?" Lindy cried.

Gazing back at them, his tongue hanging out of his mouth, prancing happily in the wet grass, the dog was running right into the path of the rumbling bulldozer.

"No, Barky!" Kris shrieked in horror. "No! Barky — no!"

25

Letting go of Mr. Wood, both girls dove toward the dog. Hands outstretched, they slid on their stomachs on the wet grass.

Unaware of any problem, enjoying the game of tag, Barky scampered away.

Lindy and Kris rolled out of the path of the steamroller.

"Hey — get away from there!" the angry operator shouted through the high window of the steamroller. "Are you girls crazy?"

They leapt to their feet and turned back to Mr. Wood.

The rain began to come down a little harder. A jagged streak of white lightning flashed high in the sky.

"I'm free!" the dummy cried, hands raised victoriously above his head. "Now you will pay!"

"Get him!" Kris shouted to her sister.

The rain pelted their hair and shoulders. The two girls lowered their heads, leaned into the rain, and began to chase after the dummy.

Mr. Wood turned and started to run.

He never saw the other steamroller.

The gigantic black wheel rolled right over him, pushing him onto his back, then crushing him with a loud *crunch*.

A loud *hiss* rose up from under the machine, like air escaping from a large balloon.

The steamroller appeared to rock back and forth.

A strange green gas spurted up from beneath the wheel, into the air, spreading out in an eerie, mushroom-shaped cloud.

Barky stopped scampering and stood frozen in place, his eyes following the green gas as it floated up against the nearly black sky.

Lindy and Kris stared in open mouthed wonder.

Pushed by the wind and the rain, the green gas floated over them.

"Yuck! It stinks!" Lindy declared.

It smelled like rotten eggs.

Barky uttered a low whimper.

The steamroller backed up. The driver jumped out and came running toward them. He was a short, stocky man with big, muscular arms bulging out from the sleeves of his T-shirt. His face was bright red under a short, blond flattop, his eyes wide with horror.

"A kid?" he cried. "I — I ran over a kid?"

"No. He was a dummy," Kris told him. "He wasn't alive."

He stopped. His face faded from red to flour-white. He uttered a loud, grateful sigh. "Oh, man," he moaned. "Oh, man. I thought it was a kid."

He took a deep breath and let it out slowly. Then he bent to examine the area beneath his wheel. As the girls came near, they saw the remains of the dummy, crushed flat inside its jeans and flannel shirt.

"Hey, I'm real sorry," the man said, wiping his forehead with his T-shirt sleeve as he straightened up to face them. "I couldn't stop in time."

"That's okay," Kris said, a wide smile forming on her face.

"Yeah. Really. It's okay," Lindy quickly agreed.

Barky moved close to sniff the crushed dummy.

The man shook his head. "I'm so relieved. It looked like it was running. I really thought it was a kid. I was so scared."

"No. Just a dummy," Kris told him.

"Whew!" The man exhaled slowly. "Close one." His expression changed. "What are you girls doing out in the rain, anyway?"

Lindy shrugged. Kris shook her head. "Just walking the dog."

The man picked up the crushed dummy. The

head crumbled to powder as he lifted it. "You want this thing?"

"You can throw it in the trash," Kris told him.

"Better get out of the rain," he told them. "And don't scare me like that again."

The girls apologized, then headed back to the house. Kris cast a happy grin at her sister. Lindy grinned back.

I may grin forever, Kris thought. I'm so happy. So relieved.

They wiped their wet sneakers on the mat, then held the kitchen door open for Barky. "Wow. What a morning!" Lindy declared.

They followed the dog into the kitchen. Outside, a flash of bright lightning was followed by a roar of thunder.

"I'm drenched," Kris said. "I'm going up to get changed."

"Me, too." Lindy followed her up the stairs.

They entered their bedroom to find the window wide open, the curtains slapping wildly, rain pouring in. "Oh, no!" Kris hurried across the room to shut the window.

As she leaned over the chair to grab the window frame, Slappy reached up and grabbed her arm.

"Hey, slave — is that other guy gone?" the dummy asked in a throaty growl. "I thought he'd never leave!"

Add *more*

Goosebumps®

to your collection . . .

Here's a chilling preview of

DEEP TROUBLE

1

There I was, two hundred feet under the sea.

I was on the hunt of my life. The hunt for the Great White Stingray.

That's what they called him at Coast Guard Headquarters. But, me, I called him Joe.

The giant stingray had already stung ten swimmers. People were afraid to step into the water. Panic spread all up and down the coast.

That's why they sent for me.

William Deep, Jr., of Baltimore, Maryland.

Yes, William Deep, Jr., world-famous twelve-year-old undersea explorer. Solver of scary ocean problems.

I captured the Great White Shark that terrorized Myrtle Beach. I proved he wasn't so great!

I fought the giant octopus that ate the entire California Championship Surfing Team.

I unplugged the electric eel that sent shock waves all over Miami.

But now I faced the fight of my life. Joe, the Great White Stingray.

Somewhere down deep under the sea, he lurked.

I had everything I needed: scuba suit, flippers, mask, oxygen tank, and poison-dart gun.

Wait — did something move? Just behind that giant clam?

I raised my dart gun and waited for an attack.

Then, suddenly, my mask clouded. I couldn't breathe.

I strained for breath. No air came.

My oxygen tank! Someone must have tampered with it!

There was no time to lose. Two hundred feet down — and no air! I had to surface — fast!

I kicked my legs, desperately trying to pull myself to the surface.

Holding my breath. My lungs about to burst. I was losing strength, getting dizzy.

Would I make it? Or would I die right here, deep under the ocean, Joe the Stingray's dinner?

Panic swept over me like an ocean tide. I searched through the fogged mask for my diving partner. Where was she when I needed her?

Finally, I spotted her swimming up at the surface, near the boat.

Help me! Save me! No air! I tried to tell her, waving my arms like a maniac.

Finally she noticed me. She swam toward me and dragged my dazed and limp body to the surface.

I ripped off my mask and sucked in mouthfuls of air.

"What's your problem, Aqua Man?" she cried. "Did a jellyfish sting you?"

My diving partner is very brave. She laughs in the face of danger.

I struggled to catch my breath. "No air. Someone — cut off — tank —"

Then everything went black.

2

My diving partner shoved my head back under the water. I opened my eyes and came up sputtering.

"Get real, Billy," she said. "Can't you snorkel without acting like a total jerk?"

I sighed. She was no fun.

My "diving partner" was really just my bratty sister, Sheena. I was only pretending to be William Deep, Jr., undersea explorer.

But would it kill Sheena to go along with it just once?

My name actually *is* William Deep, Jr., but everybody calls me Billy. I'm twelve — I think I mentioned that already.

Sheena is ten. She looks like me. We both have straight black hair, but mine is short and hers goes down to her shoulders. We're both skinny, with knobby knees and elbows, and long, narrow feet. We both have dark blue eyes and thick, dark eyebrows.

Other than that, we're not alike at all.

Sheena has no imagination. She was never afraid of monsters in her closet when she was little. She didn't believe in Santa Claus or the tooth fairy, either. She loves to say, "There's no such thing."

I dove underwater and pinched Sheena's leg. *Attack of the Giant Lobster Man!*

"Stop it!" she screamed. She kicked me in the shoulder. I came up for air.

"Hey, you two," my uncle said. "Be careful down there."

My uncle stood on the deck of his sea lab boat, the *Cassandra*. He peered down at Sheena and me snorkeling nearby.

My uncle's name is George Deep, but everybody calls him Dr. D. Even my dad, who is his brother, calls him Dr. D. Maybe that's because he looks just the way a scientist should.

Dr. D. is short, thin, wears glasses and a very serious, thoughtful expression. He has curly brown hair and a bald spot at the back of his head. Anyone who saw him would say, "I bet you're a scientist."

Sheena and I were visiting Dr. D. on the *Cassandra*. Every year our parents let us spend our summer vacation with Dr. D. It sure beats hanging out at home. This summer, we were anchored just off a tiny island called Ilandra, in the Caribbean Sea.

Dr. D. is a marine biologist. He specializes in tropical marine life. He studies the habits of tropical fish and looks for new kinds of ocean plants and fish that haven't been discovered yet.

The *Cassandra* is a big and sturdy boat. It is about fifty feet long. Dr. D. uses most of the space for labs and research rooms. Up on deck is a cockpit, where he steers the boat. He keeps a dinghy tied to the starboard, or right side of the deck, and a huge glass tank on the port, or left side.

Sometimes Dr. D. catches very big fish and keeps them temporarily in the glass tank — usually just long enough to tag the fish for research, or care for them if they are sick or injured.

The rest of the deck is open space, good for playing catch or sunbathing.

Dr. D.'s research takes him all over the world. He isn't married and doesn't have any kids. He says he's too busy staring at fish.

But he likes kids. That's why he invites me and Sheena to visit him every summer.

"Stick close together, kids," Dr. D. said. "And don't swim off too far. Especially you, Billy."

He narrowed his eyes at me. That's his "I mean it" look. He never narrows his eyes at Sheena.

"There've been reports of some shark sightings in the area," he said.

"Sharks! Wow!" I cried.

Dr. D. frowned at me. "Billy," he said. "This is

serious. Don't leave the boat. And don't go near the reef."

I knew he was going to say that.

Clamshell Reef is a long, red coral reef just a few hundred yards away from where we were anchored. I'd been dying to explore it ever since we got there.

"Don't worry about me, Dr. D.," I called up to him. "I won't get into trouble."

Sheena muttered under her breath, "Yeah," right."

I reached out to give her another lobster pinch, but she dove under water.

"Good," said Dr. D. "Now don't forget — if you see a shark fin, try not to splash around a lot. Movement will attract it. Just slowly, steadily return to the boat."

"We won't forget," said Sheena, who had come up behind me, splashing like crazy.

I couldn't help feeling just a little bit excited. I'd always wanted to see a real, live shark.

I'd seen sharks at the aquarium, of course. But they were trapped in a glass tank, where they just swam around restlessly, perfectly harmless.

Not very exciting.

I wanted to spot a shark's fin on the horizon, floating over the water, closer, closer, heading right for us. . . .

In other words, I wanted adventure.

The *Cassandra* was anchored out in the ocean, a few hundred yards away from Clamshell Reef. The reef surrounded the island. Between the reef and the island stretched a beautiful lagoon.

Nothing was going to stop me from exploring that lagoon — no matter what Dr. D. said.

"Come on, Billy," Sheena called, adjusting her mask. "Let's check out that school of fish."

She pointed to a patch of tiny ripples in the water near the bow of the boat. She slid the mouthpiece into her mouth and lowered her head into the water. I followed her to the ripples.

Soon Sheena and I were surrounded by hundreds of tiny, neon-blue fish.

Underwater, I always felt as if I were in a faraway world. Breathing through the snorkel, I could live down here with the fish and the dolphins, I thought. After a while, maybe I would grow flippers and a fin.

The tiny blue fish began to swim away, and I swam with them. They were so great-looking! I didn't want them to leave me behind.

Suddenly, the fish all darted from view. I tried to follow, but they were too fast.

They had vanished!

Had something scared them away!

I glanced around. Clumps of seaweed floated near the surface. Then I saw a flash of red.

I floated closer, peering through the mask. A

few yards ahead of me I saw bumpy red forma-
tions. Red coral.

Oh, no. I thought. Clamshell Reef. Dr. D. told
me not to swim this far.

I began to turn around. I knew I should swim
back to the boat.

But I was tempted to stay and explore a little.
After all, I was already there.

The reef looked like a red sand castle, filled with
underwater caves and tunnels. Small fish darted
in and out of them. The fish were bright yellow
and blue.

Maybe I could swim over and explore one of those
tunnels, I thought. How dangerous could it be?

Suddenly, I felt something brush against my
leg. It tickled and sent a tingle up my leg.

A fish?

I glanced around, but I didn't see anything.

Then I felt it again.

A tingling against my leg.

And then it clutched me.

Again I turned to see what it was. Again I saw
nothing.

My heart began to race. I knew it was probably
nothing dangerous. But I wished I could see it.

I turned and started back for the boat, kicking
hard.

But something grabbed my right leg — and
held on!

I froze in fear. Then I frantically kicked my leg as hard as I could.

Let go! Let go of me!

I couldn't see it — and I couldn't pull free!

The water churned and tossed as I kicked with all my strength.

Overcome with terror, I lifted my head out of the water and choked out a weak cry: "Help!"

But it was no use.

Whatever it was, it kept pulling me down. Down.

Down to the bottom of the sea.

3

"Help!" I cried out again. "Sheena! Dr. D.!"

I was dragged below the surface again. I felt the slimy tentacle tighten around my ankle.

As I sank underwater, I turned — and saw it.

It loomed huge and dark.

A sea monster!

Through the churning waters, it glared at me with one giant brown eye. The terrifying creature floated underwater like an enormous, dark green balloon. Its mouth opened in a silent cry, revealing two rows of jagged, sharp teeth.

An enormous octopus! But it had at least *twelve* tentacles!

Twelve long, slimy tentacles. One was wrapped around my ankle. Another one slid toward me.

NO!

My arms thrashed the water.

I gulped in mouthfuls of air.

I struggled to the surface — but the huge creature dragged me down again.

I couldn't believe it. As I sank, scenes from my life actually flashed before my eyes.

I saw my parents, waving to me as I boarded the yellow school bus for my first day of school.

Mom and Dad! I'll never see them again!

What a way to go, I thought. Killed by a sea monster!

No one will believe it.

Everything started to turn red. I felt dizzy, weak.

But something was pulling me, pulling me up.

Up to the surface. Away from the tentacled monster.

I opened my eyes, choking and sputtering.

I stared up at Dr. D.!

"Billy! Are you all right?" Dr. D. studied me with concern.

I coughed and nodded. I kicked my right leg. The slimy tentacle was gone.

The dark creature had vanished.

"I heard you screaming and saw you thrashing about," said Dr. D. "I swam over from the boat as fast as I could. What happened?"

Dr. D. had a yellow life jacket over his shoulders. He slipped a rubber lifesaver ring over my head. I floated easily now, the life ring under my arms.

I had lost my flippers in the struggle. My mask and snorkel dangled around my neck.

Sheena swam over and floated beside me, treading water.

"It grabbed my leg!" I cried breathlessly. "It tried to pull me under!"

"What grabbed your leg, Billy?" asked Dr. D. "I don't see anything around here —"

"It was a sea monster," I told him. "A huge one! I felt its slimy tentacle, grabbing my leg. . . . *Ouch!*"

Something pinched my toe.

"It's back!" I shrieked in horror.

Sheena popped out of the water and shook her wet hair, laughing.

"That was me, you dork!" she cried.

"Billy, Billy," Dr. D. murmured. "You and your wild imagination." He shook his head. "You nearly scared me to death. Please — don't ever do that again. Your leg probably got tangled in a piece of seaweed, that's all."

"But — but —!" I sputtered.

He dipped his hand in the water and pulled up a handful of slimy green strings. "There's seaweed everywhere."

"But I saw it!" I shouted. "I saw its tentacles, its big, pointy teeth!"

"There's no such thing as sea monsters," said Sheena. Miss Know-It-All.

"Let's discuss it on the boat," my uncle said, dropping the clump of seaweed back in the water. "Come on. Swim back with me. And stay away from the reef. Swim around it."

He turned around and started swimming toward the *Cassandra*. I saw that the sea monster had pulled me into the lagoon. The reef lay between us and the boat. But there was a break in the reef we could swim through.

I followed them, thinking angry thoughts.

Why didn't they believe me?

I had seen the creature grab my leg. It wasn't a stupid clump of seaweed. It wasn't my imagination.

I was determined to prove them wrong. I'd find that creature and show it to them myself — someday. But not today.

Now I was ready to get back to the safety of the boat.

I swam up to Sheena and called, "Race you to the boat."

"Last one there is a chocolate-covered jellyfish!" she cried.

Sheena can't refuse a race. She started speeding toward the boat, but I caught her by the arm.

"Wait," I said. "No fair. You're wearing flippers. Take them off."

"Too bad!" she cried, and pulled away. "See you

at the boat!" I watched her splash away, building a good lead.

She's not going to win, I decided.

I stared at the reef up ahead.

It would be faster just to swim over the reef. A shortcut.

I turned and started to swim straight toward the red coral.

"Billy! Get back here!" Dr. D. shouted.

I pretended I didn't hear him.

The reef loomed ahead. I was almost there.

I saw Sheena splashing ahead of me. I kicked extra-hard. I knew she'd never have the guts to swim over the reef. She'd swim around the end of it. I would cut through and beat her.

But my arms suddenly began to ache. I wasn't used to swimming so far.

Maybe I can stop at the reef and rest my arms for a second, I thought.

I reached the reef. I turned around. Sheena was swimming to the left, around the reef. I figured I had a few seconds to rest.

I stepped onto the red coral reef —

— and screamed in horror!

About the Author

R.L. STINE is the author of the series *Fear Street*, *Nightmare Room*, *Give Yourself Goosebumps*, and the phenomenally successful *Goosebumps*. His thrilling teen titles have sold more than 250 million copies internationally — enough to earn him a spot in the *Guinness Book of World Records*! Mr. Stine lives in New York City with his wife, Jane, and his son, Matt.

Thrills and chills to make your skin crawl... Don't you want to collect them all?

Goosebumps®

- ❏ The Abominable Snowman of Pasadena
- ❏ The Barking Ghost
- ❏ The Cuckoo Clock of Doom
- ❏ The Curse of the Mummy's Tomb
- ❏ Deep Trouble
- ❏ Egg Monsters from Mars
- ❏ Ghost Beach
- ❏ Ghost Camp
- ❏ The Ghost Next Door
- ❏ The Haunted Mask
- ❏ The Horror at Camp Jellyjam
- ❏ How I Got My Shrunken Head
- ❏ How to Kill a Monster

- ❏ It Came from Beneath the Sink!
- ❏ Let's Get Invisible!
- ❏ Monster Blood
- ❏ Night of the Living Dummy
- ❏ One Day at HorrorLand
- ❏ Say Cheese and Die!
- ❏ The Scarecrow Walks at Midnight
- ❏ A Shocker on Shock Street
- ❏ Stay Out of the Basement
- ❏ Welcome to Camp Nightmare
- ❏ Welcome to Dead House
- ❏ The Werewolf of Fever Swamp

Available Wherever Books Are Sold

◣◣ SCHOLASTIC